Christopher Krovatin

Scholastic Inc.

ISBN 978-1-339-01994-9

10 9 8 7 6 5 4 3 2 1   24 25 26 27 28

Printed in the U.S.A.   40

First printing 2024

Book design by Maithili Joshi

DEDICATED TO THE ONLY PERSON I
KNOW WHO WOULD ACTUALLY USE
THEIR SUPERPOWERS TO MAKE THE
WORLD A BETTER PLACE.

I BELIEVE IN JOHN CHEEVER.

1

RUDE AWAKENING

This time, he knows.

The kitchen smells incredible, a cozy cloud of garlic and onions and ground beef. Everyone's in a good mood for the first time in weeks. Mom looks a little less tired as she pours spaghetti and boiling water into the colander in a column of steam. Dad tosses the salad, singing what he calls "the pasta song."

Aly's there, too, at the table. Smiling, for the first time in forever. Her hair's out of her face as she laughs and shakes her head at their dad. His heart feels full and warm, and all the stirring in his mind quiets down for a bit.

Only . . . as Mom passes out bowls of pasta heaped with Bolognese sauce, he can already feel the warmth and sweetness fading.

His eyes fly to the smoke detector overhead.

His mind lights up. Something hot, nearby. Someone with a bad cloud around them, a burning mind full of bitterness and determination and smoke.

Oh no, not again, he thinks. *Please never again, someone please help, oh no oh no oh no*

"Wait," he says, his lips numb, reciting the same single word he'd said the night everything went wrong.

Mom pauses, about to sit down. Dad stops, a spoonful of Parmesan cheese hovering over his bowl. Aly's smile, her rare, wonderful smile, slowly drops into a frown.

"Simon," she says, "what is it?"

The smoke detector blares. Mom looks at the stove. Dad stands, his chair pulling out on its own. He sniffs the air. Simon gets up and runs, following the sensation in his head.

The front door is on fire. Orange and yellow light flows up from the crack at its bottom and engulfs it.

The door falls forward like the drawbridge of a castle. Lands with a boom. A cloud of fire flows in after it, swirling through the air.

And there she is, in the middle of it all.

Smiling.

Happy.

And she says—

"Come on, Theland!"

WHAP!

Simon snorted, jerked up, sat back in his chair. Mr. Roth, lanky and smirking, stared down at him from over his reading glasses, rapping the edge of Simon's desk with a copy of *Johnny Tremain*.

"I didn't realize one of the greatest works of American literature was boring enough to put you to sleep," he said.

Simon blinked away the fog and resituated himself. English class. Eraser-shaving smells, off-yellow walls. All of his new classmates stared at him silently. Judging, watching, wondering what was wrong with the new kid.

"Sorry, Mr. Roth," mumbled Simon. "Guess I dozed off."

"This is the third time you've fallen asleep in my

class, and you've only been at this school two months," Mr. Roth snapped, twisting the paperback book in his hand like he was looking at a bad dog. "This is not good, Mr. Theland. Not good at all."

A sour feeling filled Simon's mind. *Look at this guy, making this big production out of the new kid.*

"You can call me Simon," he said.

The other kids giggled at the remark. Mr. Roth's smirk went hard around the edges.

"I'd rather just call your parents and let them know there's another strike on your record, *Mr. Theland*," he said, turning away from the desk.

Simon's classmates murmured, "Ooooh . . ."

As the teacher walked back to the head of the room, Simon concentrated on Mr. Roth's mind. Something near the back of his throat and the base of his skull flexed.

The cloud of Mr. Roth's thoughts and feelings opened up in his mind's eye. Smug satisfaction. Brittle anger at being talked back to. A deep resentment toward children, unfamiliar ones especially. Excitement at Simon's possible suspension, anticipation of the looks on his parents' faces when he got reported, of seeing Simon broken, head bowed, answering him with a *yes, sir.*

Not this time, thought Simon. He'd promised himself

that at this school, he wasn't going to take it anymore.

"Now, class, as you remember from last night's reading," continued Mr. Roth, "what Esther Forbes wants you to hear is—"

Simon felt around Mr. Roth's mind, locked in on the right part, and pushed.

Mr. Roth's hand swung up. In an instant, the book was jammed in his mouth, muffling his words. The entire class gasped.

Simon let go, not wanting the teacher to choke. He glanced around at his classmates, hoping for pointed fingers, teasing laughter, some kind of public payback . . . but all he saw were frightened faces. As Mr. Roth pulled the spit-covered book from his mouth, one of Simon's classmates, Emily Grossman, stood up to help him. Mr. Roth blinked, frightened, and dropped the book like it was red-hot. Mercifully, the bell rang.

As Simon left the classroom, he dragged the back of his hand under his nose.

No blood. Not even an orange smear.

He was getting better at this.

He scarfed lunch alone, as always—pretty good rice and beans, which seemed to be the one plus side to moving to the Southwest—and then headed outside for the rest of his free period. Plenty of his classmates hung out on the old, dusty playground equipment in the schoolyard, while others sat on the benches along the fence that lined the basketball courts, looking at one another's phones and talking. Simon thought of approaching a couple of the kids from his class, saying, *What's up* . . . but when they saw him, they covered their mouths and whispered, *It's him. That new kid that all the weird stuff happens around.* At least that's what he thought he heard. Maybe Aly was making him paranoid. Eventually, he wandered off to the edge of the fence and stared out at the mountains.

New Mexico. It was so unlike his hometown—no bushy trees, no ponds or lakes, just scraggly red dirt and prickly-looking bushes for miles. Even the other places where his family had lived over the past year and a half—from Pennsylvania to Chicago to Texas to Iowa—had nothing on this Martian landscape. All the houses were small adobe squares that looked like someone had coated shoeboxes with red clay, with the Sandia Mountains looming menacingly in the distance. When he'd heard there were mountains, he'd expected snowy peaks covered with pine trees.

This looked like a giant had built a sandcastle.

He sighed. At least they were far away from home. And from Rachael.

That was what was important. Aly always told him, "Nothing matters but staying safe and making sure she can't find us."

Even if that meant being alone in the wasteland . . .

"Zombie. I'm talking to you."

Anger in the voice. He knew he should mind his own business, but his eyes followed the sound.

There, at the opposite corner of the fencing. A rangy boy and a girl stared down at another girl, with a curly bob and tons of freckles. He'd seen the two standing, and had heard about them around school—the Franklin twins, Ariana and Kirk. Tough kids, from out in the hills. The girl they were talking to was Lena Oneiro, who was in his history class. People called her Lena the Zombie because of her expressionless face and slow walk.

Lena sat with a paper bag in her lap, slowly chewing a bite of sandwich. She didn't look up at the twins, just stared straight ahead, munching away.

"Are you deaf *and* super creepy?" Ariana asked. She snatched the triangle of sandwich out of Lena's hand and tossed it away. Lena never budged.

"Must be totally brain-dead," said Kirk. "Let me try." He leaned down close to her and barked, "GIVE. US. YOUR. CHIPS. ZOMBIE. DO. YOU. UNDERSTAND?"

"Man, she's a mess," Ariana commented. She kicked red dirt onto Lena's crossed legs. Lena blinked, dust obviously getting in her eyes. But she barely flinched.

This was enough for Simon. He'd been that kid. Frozen in the face of bullies. Unable to even move.

Not at this school.

"Hey," he said, walking over to them. The twins looked up, and he saw worry cross their faces. That was good. That meant they'd heard about him.

"Mind your own business," said Kirk. He stepped forward and held up his hand—but, Simon noticed, he didn't face up against Simon, even though Simon was at least a head shorter than him. His old bully Bentley would've just grabbed him by the collar.

They were scared.

He tried not to like that so much.

"Can I ask you something?" he said. "As twins, do you guys *have* to hang out together, or are you so bad at making real friends that you're just stuck together?"

Kirk chuckled without a smile. Ariana turned away from Lena, lips curling into a snarl.

That one must have struck a nerve, Simon thought.

"That's it—I don't care what anyone says about you," Kirk muttered.

"Take him out, Kirk," said Ariana.

Kirk's hand snapped out. Grabbed Simon's shoulder. Hard.

Simon found their minds with his . . . and squeezed.

Kirk's hand flew from Simon's shoulder and up to his own temple. He and Ariana fell to their knees, clutching at their heads, letting out squawking cries of pain. Somewhere inside himself, Simon felt the urge to take it further, to push harder, make them beg forgiveness.

Then he thought about how that sounded, and let go of their minds.

"Get out of here," he commanded. The Franklin twins scrambled to their feet and left, but not before Ariana snapped "FREAK" at him.

When Simon turned to Lena, her face was still relatively frozen—but her eyes were wider than usual, and they were locked on him.

"Are you okay?" Simon asked. She nodded. "Those guys won't pick on you anymore."

Lena shrugged.

Man, what is going on with her? Simon thought. Out of habit, he reached his mind out to hers, to get a sense of her thoughts, her intentions, and—

endless

Simon blinked. He took a step backward, slapped a hand to his forehead.

He'd never experienced anything so vast, so deep, as this girl's mind. She was different. She was . . .

"You're . . . you're like me," said Simon, almost without meaning to.

Lena tensed up. In an instant, she stood and started walking away without even picking up her lunch trash or brushing off her legs.

"Wait!" Simon called out, but she was already halfway across the basketball courts and on her way back into school. He considered running after her when he felt his phone buzz in his pocket. A text from Aly.

Come to my room after school, it said. *Be careful. Don't talk to anyone.*

Why? he wrote.

Her response came immediately, and Simon felt a chill dance across his skin.

There's been another fire. I think it's her.

2

NO MATTER HOW YOUR HEART IS GRIEVING

The minute the last bell rang, Simon ran out the front doors, leapt on his bike, and sped toward home. Albuquerque rushed by in a flash of red adobe houses and wooden coyote fences, nothing taller than two stories, all dusty and baked in the blazing sun through the thin air. Living close to school had been a big part of choosing their house—Mom and Dad were incredibly busy with their new jobs, and Houston had been a nightmare of traffic—but the city wasn't much for bike lanes, and more than once a car honked at Simon as he whipped down the side of the road toward home.

Even then, Simon barely noticed. His mind was being tugged in two different directions—one in fear, the other in excitement.

Another fire. I think it's her.

You're . . . you're like me.

He tossed his bike in the pebble yard of their tiny block house—Dad insisted on calling it their *casita*—and nearly dislocated his arm trying to yank open the door. He'd forgotten that their new home was a smart house and locked automatically whenever the door closed. He fumbled with his key fob, flashing it twice across the pad with its blinking, colored light. Red light. Red light. "C'MON!" he yelled, and on the third pass, it went green with a small chirp. Some smart house.

Aly's room looked almost unchanged from when they'd moved in—bare walls, unmade bed, a massive computer setup in one corner, stacks of unopened boxes scattered throughout. He waited on her bed, and after a few minutes, he heard the pad chirp and the front door open.

"Simon?" she called as she marched toward her

room. "Simon!" She rushed through her door and practically jumped when she saw him. He almost appreciated the effect. Aly's face looked hard as stone these days, he thought, and any change in her emotions was welcome.

"Good, you're here," she said, heading straight for her computer. "It's a warehouse just outside Denver."

"Hello to you, too," Simon replied. "Listen, Aly, you won't believe what happened—"

"Wait," she mumbled, then sat down and started typing. Simon watched her blast away at her keyboard, her brow furrowed, her eyes like hard glass reflecting an endless scroll of information. He missed his old sister, the middle child who was the heart of their family, who was always there to help him when he was sad or confused or couldn't find the motivation to get dressed for school. These days, she was all business. She'd gotten her braces off in Houston, something she'd been desperately looking forward to before their lives went bananas, and hadn't seemed to care.

Then again, given what had happened, he couldn't blame her.

Originally, Aly had thought she was the one who could start fires with her mind, causing a series of accidents, punishing bullies around her whenever she got angry. In her fear and confusion, she'd gone to Rachael, their older sister, for help. Rachael had done her best to teach Aly to control herself, but it hadn't worked. Aly had been torn between appreciating her awesome new powers and feeling like an outcast . . .

. . . until she figured out that *Rachael* was the one starting fires. By then, Simon had begun to notice his own telepathic powers, his ability to read the clouds of emotion and intention around people. He'd only just started learning to give people sharp shocks of pain and to control their movements when he'd realized that it was Rachael who had pyrokinesis. Not only that, but Rachael then revealed that she'd been setting Aly up the entire time, telling the world that Aly was putting people in danger so that she'd eventually take the fall for Rachael's crimes.

The whole thing culminated in Rachael trying to burn down their school after not being picked queen of the April Showers Dance. Aly and Simon had gone to the school to stop her, but it had been a disaster. Rachael was too powerful. With fire raging around them, Simon had no other choice but to push Rachael as hard as he could. He'd put her in a coma of sorts—he was lucky he hadn't killed her—and she'd ended up catatonic in a hospital, staring at the walls without end.

For a while, anyway.

Then, during their pasta dinner, Rachael had shown up and burned down their house. That night, they found out she'd burned the entire hospital down. The police couldn't catch her.

The family relocated, hoping that Rachael would be caught. And that they'd stay off her radar in the meantime.

But she found them. Again. And again. And—

"Here," said Aly, pointing to a newspaper story on her screen. Simon leaned in and scanned the piece: A warehouse on the outskirts of Denver had been the site of a massive fire. The blaze burned out every room except for one, where it looked like people had been living illegally. Witnesses said they'd seen a teenager around the house recently, specifically a girl with curly brown hair. The authorities expected arson.

"Burned out except for the one room," said Aly. "No death, only destruction. Just like her hideouts in the other places she's followed us to. I think she knows we're here."

"Maybe," said Simon. He knew that Aly was trustworthy—she'd become a master at Internet research after Rachael had followed them to Chicago—but he was tired of moving, of panic and U-Haul trucks and fast food. And especially after what he'd found out today, he had a deep desire to stick around. "It could be a coincidence, though. Listen, Aly, today—"

"We can't afford to think like that," Aly interrupted, shaking her head. "Rachael's smart and motivated. She found us before. She'll find us again." She bit her thumbnail and scowled. "I wish we had more help. I don't want to put too much pressure on your powers."

There—if he had any chance of telling her, it was now. "I think I found someone else today. Someone like us."

Aly froze mid-nibble. Her eyes flew up to his. "What?"

"There's a girl at my school," he explained, the excitement overflowing inside of him, until his hands shook and his voice cracked. "She's like us, Aly. She has some sort of powerful mind. I think we're not alone."

Aly blinked at him a few times. "What's she like in her mind, compared to Rachael or me?"

"I don't really know, but what I got when I reached out to her was, like, *huge*," he said, holding up his hands like he was measuring a fish he'd never actually caught. "With Rachael, it's this big, oozing crater of fire and anger, and with you, it's an impenetrable wall. But hers was like a maze that went on forever. I couldn't believe it."

"Did you feel anything harmful? Anything that could hurt us?"

"Well . . . no." A smile crept across Simon's lips.

"Then ignore her," said Aly.

"What?" Simon's heart sank, hard. His smile fell as quickly as it had shown up.

"Look, dude, I'm happy you made this discovery. And, hey, maybe it'll be important in the long run," said Aly, in that matter-of-fact tone that told Simon she was trying to let him down easy. "But right now, she's not our problem. We need to focus on the task at hand."

"Aly, are you listening to me?" How could she not be excited about this? "There are more of us!"

"Of course there are, Simon. We were totally normal people, right? We didn't grow up by a nuclear reactor, or on some sacred Druid burial ground. We're just people, right? So it stands to reason that there are a bunch of people like you and Rachael out there. People who can do incredible things. But right now, only one of them is trying to burn our family alive. That's gotta be our focus."

Simon's excitement deflated, leaving him cold and desperate. "But maybe she could help us. Help us understand our powers better."

"How?" Aly folded her hands in her lap and raised her eyebrows. "How would that help us?"

Simon opened his mouth . . . and drew a blank. It stung him even more because he knew Aly was right. Their lives were in danger. But also, of course Aly *had* to be right. All he wanted was to feel less like a freak, to find someone who could be his friend . . . and here was Aly, shutting him down because it wasn't part of the plan.

"I'm sorry, dude," she said, apparently reading the expression on his face. "I know you're looking for answers here. And I'm sure it's harder for you, given the extent of your powers. But right now, we need to protect the family. At least until Rachael is caught." She shrugged. "The greater good, you know?"

"Yeah, because this is so good. Feeling alone, like

no one can understand you. I'm so glad we're working toward this. Awesome."

Aly heaved a sigh and then put on something like a smile. "How about frozen soup dumplings for dinner tonight? I know you like those—"

"Oh, who *cares* what we eat, Aly?" Simon snapped. He walked out of the room, slamming the door behind him as hard as he could, hoping the house's computer registered just how angry he was.

3

SLEEPWALK

Dad sings, out of tune, jaunty. The pasta song.

Steam rises from the sink.

Simon looks around the kitchen. It's all happening again, just as he remembers it, only now it feels out of order. One second the pasta's in the sink, the next it's covered in sauce in front of him. Dad moves backward; the cheese rises from his bowl and nestles itself back in his spoon. Aly sits at the table, only it's different Alys, the way she's been in the other dreams and then the way she was before and then the tired-eyed teenager he sees every day these days. It's as though the memories have caused a pileup, with each one struggling to get their time in.

He knows they're all waiting. All he has to say is one word, and then the horror will start over again.

Maybe this time, he doesn't have to say it. Maybe he can hold his tongue, and the burning will never come, and they can live here, in this happy moment, forever.

But then the sensation hits. His warning sign, the searing orange sense of danger that swells in his mind. And as hard as he tries, Simon can't hold the word back, because holding it back isn't how it happened then, and he can't change his memory no matter how hard he tries. The feeling balloons with poison, and then bursts as he utters that one syllable:

"Wait."

Time corrects itself; the family is at the table, pasta in front of them. They all look at him, waiting. Aly's smile once again sours into a grimace, as though the Aly in his dreams also knows what she will unleash when she says,

"Simon, what is it?"

Smoke detector. Dad rises. Simon tells himself to hold still, to stay at the table, but he can't, he's up, he's at the front door to witness orange tongues licking its edges, and then it falls, and the fire blares, and in the center of the blaze is Rachael, smiling, happy, surrounded by fire but never burned.

She grins at him, and says, "Hey, Simon. We gotta talk."

Simon does what comes naturally. He reaches out with his mind and pushes, hard. Rachael scrunches up her face in pain and lets out a grunt. For a moment, the flames die down . . . and then she flicks out her hand, and the fire flows out, forcing Simon back with a cry.

She's stronger now, he realizes. He'll have to concentrate harder to stop her.

She might burn them all before he can.

"Run!" he yells as he bolts back into the kitchen. Mom and Dad and Aly all turn, but it's as though they're on a conveyor belt, running but getting nowhere, each second a deeper swamp of slow motion. Simon wants to help, to push them out of the house, but he can't.

He feels the hairs on the back of his neck singe.

The fridge door swings outward.

Simon gasps.

That didn't happen. It hasn't happened in any of his dreams, either.

What—

Hands snatch out of the fridge and yank him inside.

A blast of cold air, a feeling of weightlessness, a close-up on the mustard—and then he falls to the ground. Pebbles and sand stick to his palms as he scrambles, trying to figure out what's happening.

When Simon climbs to his feet, there's a beautiful view sprawled out before him, an endless display of red sand and whirling brush. He stands at the top of a mountain, staring down at an immense valley below. A splash of electric lights lies scattered on the ground, spelling out Albuquerque, his new home, seen from above. The sun sets in the distance, painting the sky a stunning mixture of burning purple and buttery yellow.

"Where am I?" he mumbles, trying to make sense of what's just happened.

"The top of the Sandia Mountains. Or at least how you picture them."

Simon turns to the voice. A girl stands a few feet away, admiring the view. She wears a red dress with a flowing skirt over brown cowboy boots. Her hair flutters in the breeze, and features a green highlight in the shape of a lightning bolt. It takes Simon a moment to realize that it's Lena, Lena the Zombie from his class, looking radiant in a way he's never seen her be.

"I thought I was in a dream," says Simon.

"You still are," she says. "It's just mine now. Or, at least, I'm in control of it."

The thought leaves him dumbfounded. He remembers how powerful her brain was when he took a look inside of it.

"So you did take a look," she says. "I thought that's what I felt."

Simon feels chilly. Caught, red-handed. "You can read my mind."

"I can do anything here," she responds with a confident smile that makes her freckles curl upward. He likes that smile, and can't help but return it.

"Is that why you saved me from my dream?" he asked. "To show me your powers?"

"No," she says. "I wanted to warn you."

"Warn me about—"

In a flash, she stands in front of him. She seizes the collar of his shirt and lifts him off the ground, and suddenly they are in the air, flying out into the southwestern sky, the mountains shrinking beneath them as they drift over the city. Simon cries out, struggles, kicks his sneakers in the open air, but can do nothing as Lena holds him up effortlessly, as though she was Superman. The sky above them blossoms with dark clouds. A crash of thunder makes him flinch and scream, while bolts of lightning flicker on all sides of them, illuminating the hard expression on Lena's face.

"Stay out of my head," says Lena. "No looking. No messing around. Whatever you can do, whatever you are, you just STAY OUT OF MY MIND."

The last words come with another crash of thunder. Simon gapes, hoping to say anything that will make her put him down.

"I wasn't trying to hurt you," he spits. "I just wanted to know."

"And what did you find out?" she asks.

His mind is blank. He wonders if there's any way out of this. Maybe it's just best to tell the truth.

"That I'm not alone," he says.

Lena freezes. Her stony expression softens, just a little.

She opens her hand. Simon screams into the open air as red sand rushes up to meet him.

THE WAKING WORLD

"How'd you sleep?"

Simon blearily looked up from his Honey Bunches of Oats. Mom stared at him over her shoulder as she washed last night's pans, and offered him a tight smile. Even though he could see the fatigue of the last year and a half in the deepening lines of her face, Simon thought she was the one holding up the best. Aly had become Battle-Ready Aly, and Dad was all work in public and, from what Simon could see in his mind, was agonizing about Rachael in private. But Mom was still always checking in with them, asking him and Aly questions about their day-to-day lives, getting dinner on the table. Simon thought it was part of growing up a middle child, that need to get things done no matter how tough or crazy life had become. Aly was like that, too.

Then again, Aly had eventually snapped, and now she was like a military strategist. And according to birth order rules, as the youngest, he was still *the baby*. He *hated* that. But he also knew that Mom needed something, someone to take care of. So he'd let it be him. For now.

"I slept okay," he told her, trying to hide the exhaustion in his voice. "Had some bad dreams, but they were different than before."

"That's good," said Mom, nodding hard. "I know you were having trouble in Texas."

Trouble. Simon smiled, but it took all of his power. They'd lived in Texas for three months, and pretty much every night he'd woken up screaming. At least then, he could sleep enough; in Chicago, he'd gotten maybe four hours a night. Zero dreams.

Unlike last night.

"I actually talked to someone yesterday," he said

absently. "A girl named Lena, from my classes."

"That's *great*!" said Mom, looking genuinely surprised. She came to the table and sat across from him, beaming. "Tell me about her. What's she like?"

"She's really quiet," he said. "She gets pushed around a bit, the way I used to. I helped her deal with a couple of jerks."

Mom's bright smile fell a little bit at the mention of bullies, but she nodded. "Okay, hon. Just a reminder that you don't have to save everyone. It's important for you to focus on the things you care about. Growing yourself as a person."

For the millionth time, Simon wished he could tell her everything. About Rachael's powers, and his own, and why they were really on the run. Mom and Dad still believed that their elder daughter was just a runaway arsonist who the police somehow couldn't catch. Then again, Mom hadn't noticed Dad making things move without touching them for their entire marriage (and neither had Dad, who somehow still hadn't registered that he could open doors and cupboards using his mind instead of his hands).

But now wasn't the time. Aly would kill him. She

called that tactic *pulling the rip cord*, and said they needed to save it until it was absolutely necessary.

"I know," said Simon. "It's just nice to meet someone I can . . . relate to."

"Fair enough," said Mom. She reached out and rubbed his shoulder. "For the record, you're doing great, kiddo. I'm really proud of you. I love you so much."

He smiled tightly. "You, too, Mom." And then, because he couldn't help it: "I'm so sorry about all this."

Mom shrugged. "There's nothing to apologize for. This is just life." Her eyes glazed over, and he watched her replay the past year and a half in her mind. "You can't change it. You can only hope it evens out after a while."

Aly marched out of her room, backpack on, ready to go. She was making toast before either of them could speak to her.

"You cool, hon?" Mom asked. It was their greeting, Simon knew. Something about both being middle children.

"I'm cool," said Aly firmly. She brought her

toast to the table, but had started eating it before she sat down.

"Did you hear, your brother's already made a friend?"

Aly's chewing slowed. She nodded. "Yeah, he mentioned that. It's nice."

"Maybe these New Mexico kids'll suit you," said Mom. "You guys will suddenly become social butterflies."

"I dunno," said Aly. She glanced pointedly at Simon. "I've just got so much work to do. We all do."

School was a fog of kids and classes. Simon drifted through it absentmindedly, his eyes always searching but never finding who he was looking for. If anyone said anything to him, he didn't remember it. If he'd taken notes in his first class, he'd forgotten them. The world felt like a smear of pastels, devoid of sharpness or bright color . . .

And then he turned a corner and there she was.

Her freckles blared. Her baggy black sweatshirt flowed. She stood above everything the way an angel or an alien might.

Simon blinked through the swarm of feelings that

filled his mind. Where was this coming from? She was still Lena, Lena the Zombie, big unseeing eyes and clothes twice her size, the same way she'd been the day before on the playground. (Had she even changed, he wondered, or were those the same clothes?) All he'd wanted out of this day was to look at her, and now that he was in her presence, he thought he might vanish.

It was the dream, he realized. When he saw her, he couldn't unsee her in the dream, in her red dress and cowboy boots, flying like a god over New Mexico. And with that memory came all of them, as vivid as real life—the wind whipping his hair, the smell of smoke and earth, the way her fist had tightened around the collar of his shirt and yanked him upward.

She slid two textbooks into her bag, turned, and walked down the hall. Simon wanted to follow her—but stopped himself. That was creepy, right? Anyway, if she didn't want him reaching out to her mind, following her around school probably wasn't a good look. He needed a game plan before he could talk to her. He wasn't even sure about being in the same room with her right now. Time to stop, and think.

He got about halfway down the hall before realizing she was heading to the class they shared.

The day's timing switched—before, it had all been a flash, but suddenly every minute felt like an hour. Simon barely absorbed any of the information he was being given—Mrs. Donner was talking about the Ancient Greeks, something about the Olympian gods—but it didn't matter. All he could do was try not to look at Lena, and then, when he felt like no one was watching, to glance at her, and wonder what her deal was.

He kept catching himself trying to reach out to her with his powers. Part of him wanted to know what was going on with her endless labyrinth of a mind, to understand what breed of mind-powered person she was. (He and Aly were still working on a good word for whatever their family was, but they hated *psychic*, and *superhuman* was so cornball.) But her command in his dreams—*STAY OUT OF MY MIND*—had been pretty firm. And anyway, now that he thought about it, maybe reaching out and using his powers to read someone's thoughts and intentions wasn't cool.

Maybe everyone should have a chance to be alone in their own head.

Besides, what if it had all been in *his* head? Last night's dream was so vivid, but dreams that felt real were common enough. What if he asked her about her cowboy boots, or her demands, and found out that none of that had ever happened? If he didn't seem creepy to her now, he certainly would then—

"Mr. Theland?"

Simon jumped. He looked up at Mrs. Donner with surprise. Noticed the entire class staring at him, waiting.

"Sorry, can you repeat that?" he said, doing his best to recover.

"Please name one of the minor Greek deities," she said. "One of the ones who isn't an Olympian."

"Uh . . ." Simon's mind raced. He'd read about this last night in his homework. C'mon, c'mon . . . "Hestia?"

Mrs. Donner smiled and nodded. "Exactly, yes. Hestia, goddess of feasts. What about you, Ms. Oneiro?" A soft sound came in response, almost a whisper. "Excuse me?"

"Morpheus," said Lena, softly, in a hoarse voice. "God of dreams."

Simon stiffened. He felt crackles of icy lightning run along his veins. Now he couldn't help but stare at Lena, dumbstruck.

He'd never heard Lena speak before today.

But that was definitely the voice he'd heard in his dream.

5

BEAUTIFUL DREAMER

She was in the same place at recess.

Simon's nerves twisted themselves in knots as he walked slowly over to where Lena sat at the far end of the schoolyard. There were so many things he wanted to say to her, but whenever he tested them out, they felt somewhere between silly and utterly insane. *You have a mind unlike any I've ever seen. I stayed out of your head today, just like you asked in my dream. My sister can control fire!*

He forced himself to walk over. He was all of five

feet away when she finally looked up at him. He froze, breathless. Oh God, what could he say? What *should* he say?

"Can I eat lunch with you?" he asked.

She stared at him a moment longer, then glanced at the spot next to her and nodded.

Simon lowered himself to the ground with his back on the fence. The two stayed silent as they ate, Simon working at his turkey sandwich while she popped grapes into her mouth from a Tupperware container. He felt her presence next to him like she might be a bomb about to explode.

He had to say something. He had to know if . . . wow, it felt so ridiculous to even think.

But he had to know.

"I . . . got your message last night," he said. "I won't do it anymore. I'll stay out."

Lena kept staring straight ahead at their classmates playing kickball and talking on the benches. She said something softly through a mouthful of grape.

"Sorry?" Simon said.

Lena swallowed and said, "Shouldn't have done it in the first place."

Simon's breath hitched.

He'd *known* it was real. Somehow, he'd known it all day. But hearing her say it confirmed it.

"When did you . . ." He tried to think of the right way to say it. "How did you do that? Visit me last night?"

"How did you look in my head?" she asked softly.

Simon nodded. That was fair. He hadn't known *when* his powers had started, he'd just started seeing his mother's thoughts and feeling that there was something strange and dangerous inside his oldest sister. And unlike Aly, he hadn't then freaked out and asked for Rachael's help. He'd experimented on his own, quietly. If there was one thing he knew about being *the baby*, it was that if you made any noise, everyone fussed over you. He wanted nothing to do with that.

"When did you first know?" he asked.

Lena looked down at her empty Tupperware, and after a moment, she said, "A few months ago. I visited my brother. And I knew where I was."

"Cool," said Simon, nodding. And then, all at once, "For me, it was like opening a door. Like, the minute I started using my, uh, my mind, I just wanted to do it all the time. Everyone has their unique, uh, it's sort of like a cloud? Around them? And I just wanted to see everyone's cloud, and know what they could do, or who they *were*. And after a while, I started going harder, getting *into* people, and then once or twice when I got angry I pushed back at them, but by that time, my sister—uh, so, back up, I have two sisters—"

Lena stood. She brushed off the seat of her shorts and put her lunch stuff back in her backpack.

"Wait," said Simon.

"I don't want to talk about it anymore," she said softly. She pulled on her backpack. "See you around." Then she was gone.

Simon gaped. What had happened? It had felt so good, finally telling someone other than Aly—and Lena had just walked away. Did she not care? Didn't *she* want to talk to somebody? To feel less alone?

A sinking feeling overwhelmed him. Maybe she just didn't want to tell *him* about it.

His food tasted sour in his mouth. Who could blame her? He was some scrawny, scraggly new kid. He looked like he didn't eat enough, and the first thing he'd ever done was peek inside her head and nearly put two kids in the hospital.

He stood and trudged back to school, his heart a

storm cloud. Maybe Aly was right. Maybe he should just focus on blending in and keeping his head down.

Inside, he turned a corner—and froze. The Franklin twins stood huddled, with Kirk's back to him. Simon took a step away . . . and then he heard them talking.

"Just calm down, Kirk. It's fine."

"I can't stop thinking about it. How does that happen?"

Ariana sighed, hard. "I don't know, okay? It just did, and we should forget it. Maybe it's a twin thing."

"I've never heard of that!" said Kirk, sounding desperate. "I've never heard of twins having the *same dream*, Ari! And definitely not the same dream where they die the same way!"

6

DREAMSCAPE

The evening was typical—New Mexican take-out dinner while Dad worked late, Aly eating as quickly as possible before receding into her room to scan the Internet. Mom asked Simon if he'd hung out with his new friend, but he stayed mostly quiet, and she quickly picked up on his bad mood. And anyway, their smart thermostat was acting up again, so she was distracted with setting up Comfort Zones on her phone.

As he brushed his teeth, Simon wondered what he could do. It had been so lonely waiting to find someone else besides Rachael who was like him, and now that she was here, she didn't want anything to do with him.

In bed, he stared at the ceiling and felt around the house with his mind.

Downstairs, Dad had just gotten home, and was feeling frustrated; he'd been working remotely while they moved around, and being back at an office was annoying. (He especially disliked someone named Kyle.) But all this was really about Rachael, he knew, and how much he missed her, and was scared for her wherever she was. He hoped she was eating okay.

Mom was feeling exhausted as she read another email from the police in their hometown, saying that leads on Rachael's whereabouts were all coming up negative. The smart thermostat thing was also nagging her, but it was one part of a bigger worry that she was letting Aly and Simon down, that their family needed *some* stability.

Aly was a blank, impenetrable wall as always.

Simon knew he should go to sleep, but on the other side of sleep lay the dream, as horrible as ever.

Then again, maybe it didn't have to be there.

Was there some way to send up a flare? Ask for a second chance?

He tried something he'd never done before: He closed his eyes, thought a single sentence, and aimed all his focus on it. He couldn't feel the same flex that came with pushing another person's mind, but he hoped it would work.

I'm here, thought Simon. *Find me if you want to.*

He released the thought into the air, then rolled over and let the pillow take him.

A sliver of light.

Simon stops, and in the oatmealy slo-mo of his dream, the rest of the family don't move, even as their arms and legs pump. His eyes lock onto the thin blade of white light that cuts through the burning scene around them. Until this moment, he hasn't realized how red his dream is, but the line of white light gives him some contrast, and he sees the flickering scarlet that covers their kitchen in his mind.

The fridge door is open. Just a crack, but enough for the light inside to come out.

He peers into it.

A face. Wide eyes, freckles.

Her eyes lock with his. Then, in a flash, she's gone.

Simon reaches out for the door handle. The inertia

of the dream fights him, and more than once he wonders if his hand will ever meet the handle. He does his best to focus only on the white light, not his scattering family or the figure wrapped in flames approaching behind him. Finally, through the sludge-thick air, he grabs the door of the fridge and pulls himself headfirst into it as though he's a swimmer entering an underwater cave.

For a second, the light is blinding. All is white.

Then he steps out into the same place he'd been last night, the sunset view spectacular, the air cool and full of wild smells.

Lena's not there. But he hears footfalls moving fast, somewhere in the distance.

A lizard skitters across the ground.

There, in the sand next to it, are footprints. They lead off across the mesa, down the other side, into a maze of huge rock formations that stretch off into the distance. Each one is more bizarre and impossible than the last, as though Dr. Seuss designed a sculpture garden in the desert.

He follows the footprints as they wind through the formations. At some point, he notices that he's following them in strange directions—straight up rock cliffs, winding down the middle of stone chimneys like corkscrews—but he doesn't let the oddness deter him.

Finally, he comes through a stone gate, and there she sits at a campfire in the middle of a sandy clearing. Overhead, the sky has turned to night, with stars splashed across it like spray paint. There are other things, too, huge planets with spinning rings around them, shooting stars and comets, all flashing across the glowing night in a slow but steady dance.

This time, she wears tuxedo tails over a frilly black dress, but the cowboy boots are still the same. She holds a marshmallow over the fire with a long, pointy stick that seems made for that purpose.

"Hey!" he says.

Her eyes snap up to his. She sighs and smiles frustratedly, as if to say, *Well, you caught me.*

"I'm surprised you made it here," she says. Same voice as in class, if a little louder and more confident.

"You left the door to my fridge open," he says, walking over to the campfire. Its warmth makes him realize that the night is chilly, and he holds his hands out to it. "I followed you through."

"That's impressive," she says. "Most people can't do that in their dreams. I didn't expect you to follow me, to be honest. Next time, I'll close the fridge door—"

She clamps her mouth shut and focuses on the fire, but Simon's heard enough. "Were you spying on me? After your whole dropping-me-to-my-death routine last night?"

"You left some kind of message. I felt it, which isn't normal. So I figured you wouldn't mind if I took a quick look, saw what was up. Besides, after yesterday, I wanted to see how your dream ends. It's a very lucid dream. I wish I knew what was going on in it."

Heat floods his cheeks, his internal temperature matching that of the fire. "I'm not sure I'm okay with that. I mean, I can't look into your mind unannounced, but you can spy on me in my dreams?"

"I don't hurt people with my powers," she says.

"What about the Franklin twins?" asks Simon, feeling strong, vindicated. "They didn't seem happy about the dream they had last night."

Lena's shoulders sag. He's got her. It's not exactly a feeling he likes. He's not trying to out her. But he's also not about to let her just spy on him while he's asleep.

"Look." Simon sits next to her by the fire. "The way I see it, there are two ways we can do this. One is, we make a hard rule to leave each other alone. No spying, no interacting—we just accept that there's someone else out there with powers like ours, but we don't question it." He hates making that an option, what with how desperate he is to know about her. But he needs to offer it after his realization that using his powers without permission isn't fair. "The other is that we come clean. Get to know each other. See what our powers can do."

Lena furrows her brow. She leans over and extends the stick to Simon.

"You don't want it?" he asks.

"Honestly, I've already had three," she says.

He pulls the browned marshmallow from it and eats. The flavor is beyond delicious, like a million different shades of caramel combining in his mouth. He's about to thank her when he sees that she has a new marshmallow speared on the end of the stick.

"A few rules, if we do this," she says.

"Okay."

"First, this is just about learning about each other's powers." Lena glares at him pointedly. "We are not going out or anything. You're not my boyfriend. If I find out you've told anyone that we're a couple, I'll make sure you regret it."

"That's not at all what I'm going for," says Simon, holding up his palms.

Lena huffs and nods. "Second, we don't talk about it at school. I don't want any more attention than I already get. And that includes coming to my rescue when some bullies act like jerks. No offense, I just . . . like my privacy."

Simon shrugs. "Fine by me."

Lena stares into the fire for a moment longer, then says, "Okay, I'm in." She extends a hand, and he shakes it. Her palm is soft and clammy. He's amazed at how real it feels.

"Cool," he says with a smile.

He can see that she's trying not to, but she smiles nonetheless. "Cool. Let's meet back here tomorrow night, and we can talk. I'll see you then."

"Can we talk now?" Simon tries.

Lena smiles. "Sorry, but I have a flight to catch."

She points a finger at the fire, then sweeps it into the air. The cluster of burning logs rises up in front of them, suspended a few feet overhead. Lena holds out her other hand, and the air seems to ripple between them. Suddenly, they're sitting in front of a hot-air balloon, its bulb decorated with yellow and red zigzags, the former campfire now filling it with heat.

Lena grabs a knotted rope dangling from the basket and swings herself in. The balloon takes off, floating out over the lights of Albuquerque.

Simon watches her go, speechless, wishing she'd stay. Then, at the last minute, she turns back to him and waves, and his heart seems to light up with a happiness he can't remember feeling in ages.

ASLEEP ON YOUR FEET

"You look tired," Aly observed the next morning. She stood in the doorway to the garage as Simon got his bike. "Have you been sleeping okay?"

Simon wanted to assure his sister that he was fine, but he wasn't that good a liar. He could feel the bags under his eyes, the weight of fatigue on his shoulders. It wasn't that he'd woken up tired, he'd just woken up at three in the morning. And then he couldn't sleep to save his life.

She'd made the hot-air balloon. Just *made* it.

"It's the new house," Simon bluffed. "I always have trouble sleeping in new places."

Aly nodded knowingly. "I remember our vacation to Delaware."

"Three days, zero sleep," groaned Simon, and they laughed.

For a second, Simon saw a flash of the old Aly, his biggest fan, who helped him get dressed and eat breakfast on the days when he just couldn't get out of bed for fear of bullies or tests or what mood Rachael would be in. He'd been so frozen by life, unsure how to do anything himself, and there was able, heartfelt Aly, never frustrated with him, always ready to lend a hand. It was nice, he thought, that their old life was still there a *little*, that the past year and a half (which felt like ten years) hadn't ruined everything.

He reached out to her mind, gently—and hit stone. Nothing, no way in, impossible to get through. Simon couldn't even peek inside. Aly's power didn't look as impressive as his and Rachael's, but her mental armor was certainly as strong as his own abilities.

"Well, look, I haven't seen any more chatter online, so that Denver fire might have been a fluke," she said. She seemed torn, like she wanted to be both her official new self and her supportive younger one. "I'm sorry if I freaked out a bit."

"It's cool," said Simon, shooting her a smile. "You're just looking out for us. You always have. You should take a break from it, like Mom says."

Take a hot-air balloon ride.

He bit his lip to keep from saying it out loud.

"Maybe I should," she said. And then, out of nowhere, "I miss Rachael sometimes. I feel like we're all, uh . . . Never mind, it's stupid."

"What's up?" he asked.

Aly huffed. "I feel like we're missing a piece as a family. We're all gears, spinning, and we're missing the one in the middle that connects us." She glanced at him. "Do you ever think about her?"

Simon thought about his oldest sister.

In his mind, he saw a column of fire.

"Every night I dream about the day she came home," he blurted.

NO. Why had he said that out loud? But it was too late—he could see the shock on Aly's face, and the roots of worry it was digging into her. She was putting it all together—the bags under his eyes, his sudden need for a friend, everything he'd said or done for the last month. And once again, he'd be a thing to be concerned about, for Aly to worry and toil over, to fuss over, *the baby*.

"Sorry, it's nothing," he mumbled, hopping on his bike and slapping the garage door opener on the wall. The opener beeped, and Simon cursed and dug out his phone to open it using the app. Aly asked him something, but the sudden drone of the door mechanism drowned her out. He rode out into the radioactive sunshine and kept his head down until he got to school.

Lena's rules had sounded easy last night, but at school they were murder. All day, Simon had to keep himself from trying to find her and talk to her. He forced himself to follow them, though; he was so curious about her powers that he couldn't risk not getting to talk to her tonight, when he was asleep.

He kept wondering if this was real. Even after Lena had talked to him about it at lunch yesterday, he'd second-guessed himself left and right. It was all so elaborate, so bizarre. Hot-air balloons out of nothing, flying out into the air and creating a lightning storm— these things were incredible, even for a telepath who had nearly put his firestarter sister in a coma. He wasn't sure he'd ever believe this was happening, no matter how often they talked about her powers in the real world.

Heck, maybe this was a dream.

Simon glanced at school around him.

A really long, boring dream.

At lunch, he saw Lena in her usual spot and considered going over to her, but was worried that would seem too aggressive. If *don't talk about it at school* was a rule, was he allowed to talk to her at all? What else would they talk about, anyway?

What else did they have in common?

Huh. Maybe that was the problem.

He made his way over to Lena and took his place next to her. Same as always, she looked briefly over at him, but stayed quiet otherwise. Simon had some of his lunch—PB and J, Mom must have been swamped—and tried to think of what to say next.

"So, uh . . . what kind of music do you listen to?" he asked.

Lena froze midway through opening a bag of chips. She blinked a few times and mouthed a few words, like she was rehearsing the part of Lena When She Answers the Question. Then she cleared her throat, ripped open the bag, and nodded slowly. Simon recognized the motion; he'd made it enough times already in his life. It said, *Here we go, now or never.*

"I like Halsey," said Lena slowly. "And Olivia Rodrigo. And my brother got me into these bands named Enter Shikari and Nova Twins. They're kind of loud and heavy for me, though." She looked at Simon. "What about you?"

Simon opened his mouth to respond . . .

Wait, now what?

"I don't know," he said. "I don't really listen to music."

Oh God.

He was the one kid on earth who didn't listen to music.

Lena stared at him for a moment, face totally blank . . . and then her mouth drew into a grin.

"Wow," she said. She started to shake with laughter. Then it spread to Simon, and he started laughing, too. They giggled uncontrollably, two minds who could do so much, realizing they knew so little.

For the rest of the day, Simon felt a hundred pounds lighter. He walked to class with his head up and a smile on his face. Once or twice, someone he passed would look at him weird; he casually overheard some kid mention that the creepy new kid looked even creepier when he smiled. But he couldn't be bothered with them.

He had talked to Lena about music all of recess. She'd given him a Spotify playlist recommendation.

He had a friend.

Had he *ever* had a friend?

In English class, he listened, and even took some notes on *Johnny Tremain*. Mr. Roth flinched when he raised his hand, but said "Good work" when he got the answer right. For the first time in as long as he could remember, he felt like a normal kid. Like he wasn't living at the bottom of some strange, shadowy hole, worried that if he poked his head out, he'd get hit.

After class, he kept his eyes out for Lena, and found her getting a drink of water at the fountain. She smiled and waved when she saw him, and if Simon didn't know any better, he'd say she was feeling the same—

A black-and-white ball smacked into the wall next to Lena's head. Both of them flinched and crouched.

"My bad!" yelled a girl from across the hall. Simon

had seen her around—Erica something, pretty popular, a year older than him, athlete. She and two others stood in green uniforms and shin guards. A soccer ball lay at Lena's feet. She stared at it silently, still in shock, trying to make sense of what was going on.

"Be more careful next time," snapped Simon, feeling stung that the moment had been shattered so quickly.

"Oooh, okay, Romeo," laughed Erica. "It was an accident, I promise. Ball got away from us." She looked at Lena. "Sorry about that, Zombie. Mind kicking that back over? We've got stuff to do."

A feeling swept over Simon in an overpowering wave. The muscles at the base of his skull bunched, and the back of his throat swelled. In fact, it felt like his whole head was swelling, like the world had turned black-and-white and silent around him and all that he could see was Erica's smirk, the cloud of arrogance around her like a poisonous gas, how easy it would be to reach into that mind and twist it in a way that would stop her from walking ever again—

Lena's hand, soft, clammy, landed on his arm.

Simon's furious momentum vanished instantly. He felt shocked, more frightened at himself than angry. How long had he been glaring at Erica?

He glanced at Lena, and she gave a barely visible shake of her head. Then she gently kicked the ball back over to Erica, who picked it up and left like nothing had happened.

"Thanks," he said, feeling the last of his uncontrollable rage dry up and blow away. It hadn't been easy, letting go of the anger. In the moment, he'd felt like . . .

How Rachael probably feels.

He tried not to think it, but the idea kept creeping into his mind. In moments like this, he couldn't help wondering—was this what it felt like to be Rachael? Was he really any different than her, on the inside?

"That's okay," Lena said softly. "Glad you stopped yourself."

Simon took a deep breath and smiled. That was the difference between him and Rachael. He'd held back. Rachael never held back.

"Talk more tonight?" he asked.

"Wouldn't miss it," she said.

8

IN YOUR DREAMS

The fridge door is open again, sending a lance of white through the red of Simon's dream.

If that was an accident last night, then tonight, it's on purpose.

In classic dream fashion, the harder he pushes his hand toward the fridge door handle, the harder it is to move. He takes a deep breath, does his best to tune out the elaborate scene around him, and takes the door handle. It opens, and he swims through.

She's on the other side, on the plateau where he

comes out. She wears black jeans, a T-shirt with her own face on it, and a leather jacket bristling with silver spikes, all above her signature cowboy boots. A few yards off, the hot-air balloon floats, tied to a post to keep it from drifting away, as if it were a balloon at a birthday party.

"Your jacket's cool," says Simon. "Why don't you ever wear stuff like that to school?"

"This? I don't own this," Lena says with a laugh. "That's the beauty of dreaming. I can wear anything in the world. One night, I wore one of those inflatable *T. rex* costumes the entire time. Just to see what it was like."

"How'd that go?"

"I fell down about fifty times."

Simon laughs, which makes her smile and blush a little. He can't believe they're having this conversation, here, inside his dreams. Then again, who knows? Maybe they aren't. Maybe he's lost his mind.

"So, can we talk about your powers here?" he asks. "I know you don't like talking about it in school, but I figure here . . ."

"Yeah, it's cool," she says. "Want to talk in the balloon? You seemed pretty impressed by it yesterday."

Why does his stomach flutter at the idea of getting into that basket? Simon knows he is dreaming. That he can't plummet to his death here, that the heights aren't real. So why is he suddenly so frightened of climbing into that basket?

"Sure," he forces himself to say.

It's just a dream, he thinks as he feels the knotted rope bite into his hands. *It's just a dream*, he thinks as he clumsily tumbles into the wicker basket, landing on his face after Lena nimbly leaps inside. *Just a dream*, he thinks as Lena flicks her hand, the rope keeping the balloon anchored comes unraveled, and they drift away from the land.

But the wind in his hair feels as real as ever, the pounding of his heart louder than ever before. He glances over the edge and feels dizzy at how far up they are. His hands grip the edge of the basket so hard his knuckles go white.

"You get used to it," says Lena, staring casually over the edge. "It's a little different for me, given what I'm able to do."

"And what is that, exactly?" asks Simon, doing his best to think through his panic and fear. "You can go into other people's dreams and control them?"

"More like shape them. I'm not exactly a wizard or something here. But I can move around existing ideas and memories, or I can insert some of my own. It's more like infiltrating a dream than controlling it. It's not as fast-acting as your power, but it lets me do cool things."

She flicks her fingers, and a piercing cry echoes out between the mountains. A few hundred feet away, a *Pteranodon* wheels through the air, its webbed wings spread wide, its scales rippling in the evening light. Simon's breath hitches at the sight of the flying dinosaur, vaguely registering that it looks exactly like the model they have at the Albuquerque Natural History Museum, where Mom took them the first week. He knows it's not real, even as the wind from its swoop flutters against his face.

"And the stuff we can see is the easy part, too," says Lena. "Ideas, emotions, concepts . . . those are the tricky bits. When people encounter an idea in a dream, it affects them in ways they might not understand. It sinks in deeper."

Simon is speechless. Partly because Lena has obviously thought about her power pretty thoroughly, and partly because this is easily the most he's ever heard her say at one time.

"And it first manifested on your brother?" asks Simon.

"That's right." Lena wraps her arms around her chest and looks away, suddenly standoffish. "He'd said something mean to me that day, and then I showed up in his dreams, and told him not to."

"What'd he say?"

Lena is silent for a moment, watching the *Pteranodon* disappear in the distance. Then she turns back to Simon. "What about your abilities? Is your power mind-reading? Is it telekinesis?"

"No telekinesis," says Simon. "That's my dad. And mine isn't exactly mind-reading, either. It's like I can see people's feelings and intentions around them in a sort of cloud. I can pick up on what they're planning to do, the ideas behind it. And then I can grab parts of their minds and push. That's what makes it hurt, or makes people do things."

"Right. But hold on. Does your whole family have powers?"

"Not my mom. But yeah. Me, my sisters, and my dad."

"That must be kind of cool," says Lena, raising her

eyebrows. "A whole family of people with incredible powers."

Simon sighs. "You'd think that, right?"

He tells her before he even means to.

It doesn't pour out of him so much as sprays, like water bursting through cracks in a dam. The minute he starts explaining his family to Lena, the past year and a half jets out of him: Rachael and him discovering their powers, Rachael trying to pin all her crimes on Aly, getting locked in Rachael's room and having to take control of the mind of a pizza boy to escape. How Rachael sat dead-eyed in a hospital for weeks . . . and then woke up with a vengeance. How she'd come for them, burned down their house, and followed them for months and months afterward. He told her about their mom trying to get the FBI on the phone and being told to wait eight weeks for her paperwork to be processed while her daughter left a trail of arson in her wake. About his dad's powers of slamming doors and adjusting the thermostat without knowing he was doing it. About his wonderful, supportive sister Aly turning her entire life into the fortress that was her mind.

After a while, Lena slides to a crouch in the basket of the balloon and listens to him. Simon knows he is going on for too long, probably telling Lena more than she wants to know. But he can't help it. He didn't know his feelings were this close to the surface, and now that they're being let out, they're not stopping.

When he's finally done, Lena sighs and says, "And I thought *my* family was hard to take."

"It's been a really tough time," Simon admits.

"So that's what's going on in your dream," Lena observes. "That girl in the fire, smiling . . . that's your sister?"

"Rachael, yeah." He rubs his face. "Maybe that's why I'm really quick to use my powers to hurt people. I'm just scared that at some point, she's going to come for me. For us."

"Maybe," says Lena. She sticks out a foot and gives Simon a slight nudge. "But I also wonder if you're just sick of being pushed around. Which makes sense. So you're showing everyone how tough you are, so they can't hurt you."

The comment stings Simon. He's just unloaded his family crisis, put his heart out in front of her . . . and Lena thinks he's trying to play tough guy?

"So making someone have a nightmare to teach them a lesson—that's okay, though?" he asked.

Lena pulls her foot back. "That's fair. I mean, I never said I was perfect. I'm just saying—"

"Yeah, I get it. Either I get stepped on by everyone around me, or I'm angry and scary. Another no-win scenario for Simon Theland. Awesome."

"I didn't mean it like that, at all." Lena smiles tightly, but Simon can tell she's upset. "I'm sorry. We can talk about this more tomorrow night, if you want."

"Oh, you don't want to talk about it now?" he asks. He knows he's overreacting, but he can't help it. Suddenly, he feels like he needs to put up his dukes. "Big surprise."

"I would talk about it tonight, but your alarm is about to go off."

"What?"

Xylophone tones. The sound of plastic vibrating on wood.

Simon rolled over and slapped his phone with a groan. Milky morning light poured in under his blinds, and the chirping of birds was audible outside his window. As much as he desperately tried to force himself back to sleep, it was no use. The dream was gone. He was up.

He sat in bed and tried to remember all the details of the dream. While he was with Lena, it all felt so real, as real as everyday life . . . but like most dreams, when he tried to remember this one, the lines seemed smeared and hard to capture.

He remembered getting angry at the end, from what she'd said. It had felt like an attack, a cruel comment while he was feeling so vulnerable. Now, thinking about it in the light of day, he understood why she'd set him off so badly:

She was right.

When was the last time he'd used his powers to do anything good? Had he ever used them to help people? All his memories of using his powers were either of self-defense or standing up to bullies. Even when using his ability to read people's "cloud," it was to gauge them as a threat or figure out the right way to hurt them. And when he'd gotten here, to his new school, he'd hardened. He'd decided that he wasn't going to take anyone's crap anymore, and lashed out whenever he felt cornered or angry.

And how was he feeling now? Any less angry? Any less cornered?

Rachael's grin appeared in his mind, surrounded by a halo of flames.

If he *was* different than his oldest sister, then he couldn't just use his powers to punish people who made him angry. He needed to *be* better, every day.

Simon got to his feet and started getting dressed. As he was pulling his shirt on, Aly stuck her head in, doing the usual parent-mandated Simon check-in in case he'd gone back to sitting on his bed half-dressed until it was time to go.

"Okay, cool, you're up," said Aly. "Ready for another exciting day at school, no doubt."

"You know," Simon replied, "today, I actually might be."

9

MEETING OF THE MINDS

There. He saw it as it was happening. He had to act fast.

The kid two rows in front of him, Jaden something, was elbowing a beaker off his lab table. He didn't know he was doing it, but as he scribbled down notes, his elbow nudged it farther and farther toward the edge of the table . . . until it began tipping over.

Simon acted fast. He reached into Jaden's mind, found what he thought—hoped—was the right nerve center, and twisted.

The boy's arm shot out, and in a flash he'd caught the beaker less than a foot from the ground. Jaden looked at the glass in his hand like it had appeared out of nowhere, while a girl at the table across the aisle from him—Simon thought her name was Molly— stared at his catch with her mouth hanging open.

Simon smiled to himself. Another success. He was trying it out all over school, helping kids avoid minor catastrophes. He'd helped kids close lockers before they spilled over, dodge basketballs flying toward their heads, and had even helped a teacher who was seconds away from pouring coffee all over one of her colleagues. His aim hadn't always been perfect—one student had jumped some two feet in the air, and twice he'd tried to get someone to use one arm and they'd used both—but so far, he was pretty skilled at making sure people did what they needed to in order to stay safe.

It felt good, he thought, doing things to help others. Each action felt kind of tiny, but Simon knew better. He was well aware of how a dropped beaker or some spilled coffee could make you feel worthless and miserable for the rest of the day.

And maybe, he told himself, if there was hope for him, there could be hope for Rachael. If he could shake off his anger and start using his powers to help people, maybe she could, too. If he could show her what he was doing to help his classmates, she could . . .

Use fire to warn them?

It sounded far-fetched for anyone, but especially for Rachael. Still, he told himself, there had to be a way. Maybe he and Rachael were different, but he wouldn't give up on her.

During recess, he waved to Lena. On his way over to her, he decided to try something new. He gently sent out with his mind, widened his own reach, and examined the various mental clouds out in the schoolyard. He could feel the other kids' emotions and understand their reasoning; the excitement of kickball and disappointment of a bad TV show episode crossed his bow at the same time.

Misery.

Someone was hurting. His eyes wandered through the crowd, trying to find who it belonged to.

They landed on Kirk Franklin.

The bully from earlier this week leaned dejectedly against a fence, glaring at his shoes. His sister bounced antsily at his side, talking, but Kirk wasn't listening. Simon could feel the self-loathing coming off Kirk in waves, and something else, too. Something more physical and personal.

Hunger.

The details of Kirk's mind unraveled for Simon as he rooted through the boy's cloud. Mom was having problems again; her new boyfriend liked to party late, and didn't care for kids. This was the third day in a row that she'd forgotten to make them a bag lunch or leave them money for something to eat. There'd be a note at home telling them to make canned pasta for dinner again, but Kirk vaguely remembered yesterday's dinner being the last can. His sister was tougher, feistier, but he just felt sick all the time. What would they do when there was nothing left to eat in the house? He'd tried cooking from that one YouTube video, and left the whole kitchen smelling like burnt onions for weeks . . .

Simon sighed. He wished it was someone else. Kirk had been *such* a creep the last time they'd interacted, and Simon had gotten too angry about it.

But the guy was hurting. His life was as upside-down as Simon's, just without visual effects.

If you're gonna be good, you've gotta try being good to everyone, Simon thought.

He took the apple out of his lunch bag and walked over to Kirk. Halfway there, Ariana spotted him coming and slapped Kirk's shoulder. The boy stood at attention, his face a mixture of frustration and fear. Ariana tensed, her fists clenching and unclenching at her sides.

"Here," said Simon, holding his lunch bag out.

Kirk eyed the bag, then squinted at Simon. "What is this?" he asked.

"It's a ham sandwich, some Ritz with peanut butter, two Hershey Kisses, and a cranberry juice," said Simon. "Yours if you want it."

Kirk froze, eyes flitting between the bag and Simon—and then his hand snapped out and snatched the bag from Simon.

Simon turned and headed over to Lena. He thought he heard one or two people whisper his name, but then realized it was a ripple across the minds around him, a flicker of acknowledgment and memory. He hadn't heard it; he'd felt it.

"Why?" asked Lena as he sat down beside her.

He shrugged, bit into his apple. "Maybe I'm just tired of thinking only about myself."

Lena handed over the bag in her hand. "You can have some of my Sun Chips."

That was all she said. It didn't bother Simon. He knew they'd talk more that night, after he went to bed.

"That was really nice of you," says Lena as they stroll through the rock formation garden. She wears a white dress covered in fluffy frills, sequins, a massive bow on the back, and steel shoulder plates like the kind you'd find on a suit of medieval armor.

"To be honest, it was what you said last night that got me thinking about it," Simon tells her. "Maybe I do only use my powers for myself, because I'm afraid. Maybe it's time I see what else I'm capable of. My sister is angry and scary . . . and that's not who I want to be."

"That's cool," says Lena. She flicks her fingers, and a team of four-inch-high cowboys on horseback goes running across their path. She smiles. "I hope you didn't think I was judging you or anything. Obviously, I've used my abilities to get back at people, too. Maybe I'll start trying something more productive, though. Planting happier ideas in people's heads."

"How do you do it?" asks Simon. "Do you just,

like, go in their dreams and throw scary thoughts at them? Monsters or car accidents or whatever's lurking in their subconscious?"

"Only when I'm making a really blunt point. If I want to give someone an idea, sink it in deep enough that it changes them, I have to be more specific. It takes some work, and sometimes some research. Like, Ms. Danaki really ripped one of my essays to shreds earlier this year, and I had to create this whole scenario where she was complimented by Principal Kleinman for being merciful to her students."

"Yikes, that sounds a lot more complicated than I expected," says Simon. They pass under a stone arch, its ceiling alive with chittering bats, and come out at the campfire. "So, you Superman-flying me out over the city and threatening me—you could've just gently planted an idea that kept me from bothering you."

Lena smiles slyly. "Some things need to be said loudly and clearly. Besides, I didn't know what you were. I was a little frightened of you."

The idea of *her* being scared of *him* makes Simon laugh. But he also remembers just how scary he'd tried to make himself when he first got to his new school. Bullies got nosebleeds, mean teachers made fools of themselves. He'd basically made himself look cursed in the eyes of everyone around him.

Maybe it's time he turns that around.

"So, I was thinking about something," he says now. "You can just go into other people's dreams, right? Whoever you want?"

"So far, yeah," says Lena, sitting down by the fire. "I think it helps if they're close by, but I haven't tested that yet. Like, I've never tried to enter into the dreams of someone in Kenya or Siberia."

"Have you ever tried to bring someone with you?" asks Simon.

"I've never had anyone here to take!" she says. "You're the first person I've ever discussed this with. I've never yanked someone out of their own dream and put them in someone else's, if that's what you're asking."

"I want to try it tonight," says Simon. "And if you can take me into someone else's dreams, I have an idea I want to plant."

"That's a massive if," says Lena. "And anyway, it's super risky. What happens when you wake up? Do you go back to your own mind? Do you stay in the one we're visiting?"

"I think that's the experiment."

Seriousness comes over Lena's face like a shadow. "This isn't a game, Simon. You seem really nice, and I don't want to put you in a coma."

"I'll be okay," he says. "My sister was in a coma once. Lasted two months, and then she felt well rested enough to try to kill our entire family."

They stand facing each other, with Lena's hands on Simon's biceps. The surreal desert landscape around them seems to go out of focus, until all he can see is the stern expression on her face. She is close to him, he thinks, closer than anyone who isn't his family has been in a long, long time. Maybe ever. He can smell her shampoo. Is that real, or part of his dream?

"Okay, take a deep breath and then just exhale, let go," says Lena.

"Let go?" asks Simon.

Lena squints. "I don't know how else to describe it. Your feet stay on the ground, but you let go of this . . . surrounding. You let yourself drift through the different dreams until you're in the one that feels right."

"Oh, great, that's not confusing or anything," says Simon.

"Let's give it a try," says Lena. She tightens her grip. "Three, two, one—"

Lena vanishes.

Simon waits. A cool mountain wind blows past.

Lena reappears in a flash.

"Okay, so that didn't work," she says, rubbing her chin. "Hmmm . . . maybe it's not possible."

"What if I use my powers?" asks Simon. "Like, in my dream, if I use my power to look into your mind, and then you travel into another person's dream?"

"Now you want us *both* to go into a coma."

"We don't have to do it if you don't want." Simon feels like he's getting a little too excited about it, and doesn't want to scare her away.

Lena looks skeptical . . . and then says, "Okay, let's give it a try."

She closes her eyes, as if she's worried it'll hurt.

Simon reaches out.

It's different in a dream—even the movements of the mind are in slow motion, like his brain is slogging through honey. And yet, in a strange way, Simon feels more of his power than he ever has before. The tension at the base of his skull feels almost kind of good, and his throat barely swells at all. It's all so smooth.

The minute he connects with Lena's mind, he feels the depth and strength of her power. Out in the waking world, looking into her head had been like staring at some massive computer motherboard, vast but cramped and tightly connected. Here, it's as though he was tapping into a huge current of raw energy. His own mind feels pleasantly seared by the size of it. For the first time, Simon realizes, he's connecting to a being more powerful than himself or his sister.

"Ready?" asks Lena.

Fear flashes through his mind unexpectedly. Should he?

"Ready," he says.

Lena takes a deep breath.

Simon falls upward.

10

DREAM JOB

It's like Lena says—flying without ever really moving.
What Simon doesn't expect is the swiftness of it, the
way the landscape of reality comes whipping around
him in various glowing clouds of people's dreaming
minds. A kitchen, a summer camp, a sedan in traffic, a
pop quiz—subconsciouses flash before him in a whirl-
wind. In a brief flickering moment between panicked
gasps of breath, Simon thinks that it's like a 3D version
of what he does, except instead of reaching into their
minds, everyone's minds are engulfing him, forcing

him to experience the sights and sounds and flavors and smells of the dreams around them.

And then, just like that, a dream lands on them and sticks. Simon stumbles back from Lena, doing his best not to look as dizzy and nauseous as he feels. The whole time, he keeps his mind connected to hers, worried that if he detaches from her brain, he'll just fall through the dreams forever.

"We're here," says Lena. She glances around. "At least I think so. Wait, look, I think that's her."

Around them looms an alley in some enormous city, brick walls on either side, the ground strewn with trash, the night sky lit purple by neon signs and strafing spotlights. A big, official-looking bouncer stands at a door in one building with a lamp over it.

Strutting toward them is a teenage girl in a short skirt and high heels, surrounded by a crew of her friends done up in varsity jackets and tight outfits. They all laugh as they follow the girl, every one of their faces declaring that they love her madly, that they are happy to be around her.

Even in a dream, Simon can see the resemblance between the Franklin twins and their mom's teenage dream-self.

"Should we hide?" asks Simon.

"They can't see or hear us," Lena answers. "I keep it that way, when I visit people. Here, watch."

The girl rolls up to the door, her crew huddling around her. She stares up at the bouncer with brazen confidence.

"Lynn Franklin and friends," she says.

The bouncer stares down at her, and slowly grows a smile so wide it seems to touch both of his ears.

"You can't come in here," the bouncer chuckles in a deep, booming voice.

"Why not?" she asks.

"Because," he says with a full laugh, "you're so OLD!"

Lynn looks down at her hands, only now they're wrinkled and gnarled, like the hands of a witch in a Halloween decoration. Suddenly, her clothes don't fit, her hair thins, and then she's a grown woman in her forties, all dressed up like a teenager, makeup smeared sloppily on her face. Her friends take notice, but instead of being concerned about her rapid aging, they all just laugh, and point, and slap their foreheads as though to say, *I can't believe I was hanging out with some old woman!*

"She's scared of getting old," says Lena. "That's so sad."

"No!" cries Lynn, running away from the door. In a blur, they're in a bedroom, and Lynn is in front of a vanity mirror, smearing handfuls of concealer and foundation on her face, doing anything she can to hide her wrinkles—but when the makeup reaches her cheek, it disappears. Soon, she's weeping, slapping at her face, desperately trying to look anything other than her age, trying to feel like the streetwise princess she used to be.

"I've got an idea," says Simon. He whispers his plan to Lena—he knows they can't be heard, but given how heartbreaking this dream is, it feels respectful to keep his voice down—and she nods in approval.

"Let me see what I can do," she says. She closes her eyes and raises an outstretched hand.

A wind whips through the room, so powerful that Lynn ducks her head and covers it with her hands. As it blows, her teenage clothes turn to dust and fall away, revealing a new outfit.

When the wind dies down, Lynn sits up and sees that she's now wearing a gorgeous golden gown, with a jeweled crown sitting atop her perfectly styled hair. She appears regal and radiant, beautiful at her own age, not pretending to be a cute teenager. A faint glow seems to emanate from her that makes the whole room look golden.

"You're so beautiful, Mom," says a voice.

Lynn turns. Ariana and Kirk stand at the doorway to the room, looking almost scared to enter.

"Yeah," says Ariana. "We're so lucky to have a mom as incredible as you."

Tears stream down Lynn's face. She spreads her arms wide, and her kids run into them. She squeezes them in a huge hug.

SIMON

"Did you hear that, too?" he asks Lena.

SIMON

A cold force grips him from behind, pulling him hard, and then he flies away from Lena, swallowed by unending blackness.

"Simon!"

A dark figure leaned over him.

He shot up, gasping for air.

The shapes of the room materialized. His desk, chair, and laptop.

Aly stood at the side of the bed, eyes barely open,

hair a tousled mess. She shushed him, a finger to her lips.

"Is everything okay?" asked Simon. "Is . . . did Rachael find us?"

"Everything's fine, dude . . . except Mom and Dad are both crying out in their sleep a lot . . . and you've got a nosebleed. Were you using your powers in your dream?"

He reached up to his nose and felt a thin slick of blood. Embarrassing, to say the least. "Yeah. I think I was. Sorry about that, Aly."

"Hey, it's all good," she said with a smile, and rapped a knuckle on the side of her head. "I didn't feel a thing. But Mom and Dad woke me up. Go clean yourself up and try to get some more sleep. We can talk about how to manage things in the morning."

"Cool," said Simon. "And I'll keep an eye on using my powers in my sleep."

"All good," she said. "It's not like you can control what happens in your dreams, right?"

The next day at recess, he met Lena at their usual spot. They said nothing, just watched and waited, anticipation building between them like an electric charge.

The Franklin twins came out of school a few minutes later. In each of their hands was a swollen paper bag. They joined another group of kids and spilled out their lunches—sandwiches, juice boxes, chips, fruit. Ariana devoured her sandwich like it was the most delicious thing in the world, while Kirk negotiated a trade with his Oreos. Both of them had a look of pride on their faces, excited to not worry over something so small as lunch.

A feeling that Simon had never really known swelled in him, bright and warm and filling. He smiled and laughed without really meaning to, as though he was so heavy with happiness he couldn't contain himself.

Simon felt cold fingers on his own, and realized that Lena had reached out and taken his hand with her free one. He linked their fingers, and together they sat and silently watched the small but powerful change they had made.

11

STAY AWAKE

The minute their silence broke, Simon went over-board. He blathered ideas at Lena in a stream of consciousness. First, it was an underground therapy team, basically using dreams to help people get over their insecurities and traumas. Then he considered how much they could make, and wondered how much kids would be willing to pay for them to go into their parents' minds and plant ideas in their dreams.

"We could do a lot of small things, you know," he told her. "Christmas present suggestions, good grades, all of that, and then we could also take on projects like this one with the Franklins where, where it's *important*, and *helps people*, and—"

"Stop," said Lena.

Simon froze, his mouth hanging open mid-word. He suddenly saw the change in Lena, how over the course of his rant she'd hunched her shoulders and hugged her chest and started glancing around at the other kids in the hallway as they entered school.

"This is a bad idea," she mumbled, shaking her head like the very idea of being revealed made her frightened. "You're talking about messing with people's lives. Their minds. And anyway, I don't want anyone to know about me and what I can do."

"We don't reveal our methods," Simon told her as they walked to her locker. "But come on, we helped someone today. We used our powers in a way that makes people better."

"You're right, and it was really good," said Lena. "But that doesn't mean we can do whatever we want. That's not okay."

"I get what you're saying—"

"I don't want to talk about it here," snapped Lena. "Rule two. Remember?"

"How can you not want to talk about it?" asked Simon with a laugh. "There's something here, Lena! Something we can do to make people happy, and to make their lives better. Aren't you sick of just playing wizard in your dreams?"

"Stop, please," she mumbled, shaking her head harder. She opened the door of her locker in his face, blocking his view of her.

Simon knew he should drop it, but her attitude stung him. Why was she shutting him out, after they'd just done such an incredible thing? Why was she okay sharing their ideas and lives together in their dreams, but the minute he wanted to do something real, that could actually affect people's lives, she clammed up? It felt mean to him. It felt unfair, to create something so cool and perfect and then be treated like he wasn't allowed into her world.

"Wow, okay," he said, throwing up his hands. "Guess I'll wait until tonight, since none of this matters to you while you're awake." He turned and started walking away.

"Simon, wait," she said.

"I thought we weren't talking about it now!" he said, trying to keep his voice from cracking.

Her mouth snapped shut, and she looked down at her shoes.

His head was a mess the whole bike ride home. Thoughts and feelings ricocheted around, colliding at random. Until Simon had come along, Lena had just been giving people nightmares when they called her names. He'd been there for her, just like she was there for him. Didn't that count for anything—

A car horn blared. A blur of red pickup truck rushed up next to him.

Simon panicked, swerved right, skidded, and fell onto his side in the dirt and trash along the shoulder of the road. His knee scraped against the asphalt, the top layer of skin peeling away.

The truck raced past him. A snickering woman leaned out of the passenger-side window and yelled, "STAY IN YOUR LANE, KID!"

Simon gritted his teeth hard. His panic, fear, and pain funneled into his anger and hurt from earlier today. The whole thing crashed down in his heart with a boom.

He reached out. Found the driver's mind.

Pushed, hard.

The pickup swerved, nearly crashing into a tree

by the side of the road. Simon could hear the woman in the passenger seat scream.

Even though he knew he shouldn't, Simon smiled. She was scared? *GOOD*. That'll teach them to . . .

. . . to . . .

I was a little frightened by you.

Lena's words echoed in his head and left a sour taste in his mouth.

What was he doing? He could've killed someone.

He let go of the guy behind the pickup's wheel and climbed to his feet. His scraped knee stung like crazy. He watched the blood bead up on it, wondering how he could nearly cause a car crash over such a small wound.

Mom's and Dad's cars were both outside when he got home, and he heard them talking in raised voices as he walked through the door. He tried to keep from eavesdropping, but the new house had thin walls, and the conversation found its way into the kitchen while he got a glass of water.

"But how *much* longer?" bellowed Dad. "It's been two weeks since you've told us *anything* important!"

A pause. "No, please, explain to me, how can *THIS* many police departments be *THIS* useless?"

Ah. It was their scheduled call about Rachael. Once again, Dad was at top intensity. He'd always had a special connection with Rachael, a real sweet emotional bond that neither of them seemed to share with everyone else. Dad was super busy and driven, and Rachael had always been obsessed with looking cool and chic, but she had always been the first to jump into his arms when they got home from school. In turn, Dad loved and nurtured Rachael's toughness and confidence, pushing her to be herself. Simon wondered if it was because Rachael was first, that she'd broken the seal for Dad and had taught him new things about himself by making him a father.

"As a matter of fact, I DO actually want you to answer that question!" Dad yelled.

Simon winced at the sound of the anger in his father's voice. He knew that Dad missed Rachael, his daughter, his friend. He wanted her back. Wanted their old life back.

What he didn't know was that their old life was gone. Rachael had burned it down. She wasn't the little girl he remembered anymore. She was something deadly.

"Derek, give me back the phone," Mom ordered.

"That's not acceptable—what—you can't just—because you're working with the *FBI*! How can you *not know where she is*?"

"Derek. Let me talk to him."

"I will in a minute."

"Then just take a deep breath—"

"YOU take a deep—sorry, what? But how much . . . you just . . . WHERE IS MY DAUGHTER?" roared Dad, making Simon's shoulders involuntarily hunch. "HOW MANY BUILDINGS DOES SHE HAVE TO BURN DOWN BEFORE YOU ACTUALLY *DO* SOMETHING—"

Dad let out a final bellow, and something heavy crashed to the ground in his parents' bedroom. Simon sipped his water, stared down at the counter. He didn't need to use his powers to know exactly what his father was feeling. His heart felt like a bottomless pit just listening to it.

He heard the door open and close, and footsteps come marching down the hall. Dad stormed into the kitchen, mumbling furious threats under his breath—and then he caught sight of Simon and froze. Simon waved weakly, barely looking up. He felt somehow embarrassed, as though he was eavesdropping on something private rather than just coming home from school. But the look of both panic and pity on Dad's face told Simon that he was thinking the same thing.

"Hey, my dude," Dad said. One of the stools at their kitchen counter pulled out on its own, and Dad sat in it without noticing. Simon wondered how much Dad was using his telekinesis these days, whether it had progressed from cupboard doors and coffee mugs to driving and typing. Would he ever realize that he was doing it?

"Sorry you had to hear that," he said.

Simon shrugged. "It's okay. So they haven't found out anything about Rachael yet?"

"Well, they're still . . . No, you know what, let's not even talk about it." Dad ran his hands through his hair, wiped under his eyes, and looked up at Simon with a forced smile. "How was school today?"

"It was okay," Simon lied. His heart was a churning mess of anger and bad feelings, and all he wanted to do was tell someone about it . . . but he couldn't be a burden now. Not when his parents were trying so hard to hold it together. Not when their entire lives felt like they were hanging on by a thread that Rachael could set on fire at any time.

"Yeah?" asked Dad. "Mom said you have a new friend. A girl, right?"

"Yeah," said Simon.

"A girl *friend*?" asked Dad.

"It's not like that," said Simon. Was it? He didn't think so. That was rule one, right? But thinking about the way they'd acted together in the dream, he wasn't sure. Did Lena holding his hand at lunch change things? How did any of that even work? "She's cool, but, like, maybe . . . maybe I think we're better friends than she does."

Dad gave him a warm, knowing smile. "I know that feeling. Like you feel you're putting your whole heart out there, and she's only giving you bits and pieces."

Simon wasn't sure about the whole heart part. But maybe a piece of it?

"It's a little like that," he said.

"Your mom was that way with me," Dad replied. "I kept wishing I could see inside her head and just knock down the walls in my way and show her how much she meant to me. But if you love . . . Well, let's say *want to be friends with someone*—I'm not trying to freak you out. But if you want to be friends with someone, it's about giving them time and space. Finding ways around the walls instead of breaking them down—or even better, convincing them that they can break down the walls on their own. You know?"

Something about Dad's comment clicked in Simon's head. He couldn't believe he hadn't thought of it before. He'd always assumed . . . Anyway, it didn't matter. Tonight, he'd ask her. It would be great. He couldn't wait.

"Yeah," said Simon. He smiled. "Thanks, Dad."

Dad looked confused, if proud. "Sure thing, kiddo. But I don't know if I did anything."

"Just for listening."

"Anytime. Hey, there's apparently a street fair going on this weekend. Why don't we all go? You could bring your new friend."

"Maybe I will," said Simon, suddenly feeling excited for the night ahead. "I'll ask her tonight."

"Oh, do you guys talk on the phone after school?" asked Dad. "Or online?"

"Something like that," mumbled Simon.

12

BROKEN DREAMS

Simon nearly sprints through the dining room as Rachael comes blazing into the house. He knows he has to move, so he bolts with the rest of the family after he says, "Run."

Then he leaps into the refrigerator the first chance he gets.

Out on the mesa, he hurries toward Lena. He's excited to tell her his idea . . . but immediately, he notices that something is off. Lena wears a turtleneck, vest, and pants, which look more subdued than her usual outfits. The balloon is here again, a ways off, but its basket rests on the ground. The city can be seen in the distance, but the lights are out. It's as though everything in this place is turned down a few notches.

"Hey," says Simon. He doesn't want to ask outright what's going on, but he remembers his father's advice and looks for a way around that question. "I like your outfit. It's different."

Lena takes a deep breath. "Look, Simon, I've thought a lot about it, and I'm not sure I want us to go into people's dreams and influence them."

Simon nods slowly. "I get why you're feeling that way."

"We're still figuring out the extent of our powers, and I'm worried that we could do more harm than good. Like, I know we helped the Franklin twins, but I did also give them a horrible nightmare after they made fun of me. And, truth be told, I feel terrible about that. So maybe it's time we just hang out, and have fun, and not make this a big mission for the good of humanity, or whatever."

Simon does his best to hold back his excitement. "I totally get it."

"You do?" A smile creeps across Lena's face. A few

lights begin to twinkle on in the city below. "Thank you for understanding. I was worried after today that you'd be angry about it."

"I was angry today because I was thinking about this the wrong way. I realized that we're friends, and I told you everything about my life, and then all I did was ask you to use your powers. And that's not fair. You're more than just a set of powers."

"That's huge of you to say," she says. "Thanks, Simon. I was so scared."

"What I was thinking is that I need to know you more, or better," he goes on before he can stop himself. "And I realized that this—" He waves an arm across the landscape. "This isn't your dream, right? This is, like, a training room. It's something you made in my dreams so we can talk alone."

"Yeah. I just call it the Mesa. It's sort of my testing area. It's easy to manifest in other people's dreams, especially if they're also from Albuquerque."

"So what I'm thinking is, let's not go into anyone else's dreams," says Simon. "Let's go into yours."

Lena's face falls. Her shoulders sag. "What?"

"I figure, all I do is tell you about me, who I am, what I want to do—it's really one-sided. Why don't we take a night in your dreams? You can show me what you—"

"No," Lena interrupts.

"Well, wait," says Simon. "Obviously, you'd still be in control."

"I said no." Lena's voice booms a little, echoing around them. She claps a hand to her mouth, then shakes her head hard. "I don't want to do that. Please don't ask me to do that."

"Why not?" Simon asks. "I'm not going to mess with your dreams or anything. I just figured that was the easiest way for you to show me who you are."

"It's nothing personal, Simon," she said firmly. "I just don't want you inside my head. I don't want *anyone* in my head. I told you that the first time. It's one of my conditions."

"No, your conditions were that we're not dating, and—"

"Then it's one of the conditions now," she snapped.

Simon flaps his lips, trying to find the right words. He hadn't expected this. He was ready for Lena to feel weird about infiltrating other people's dreams. But he'd thought that she would be excited about them just opening up to each other.

Go around the wall, Dad had said. He had to be patient.

"Then maybe, let's just talk more in the real world," Simon says. "I guess I just feel like we only talk during dreams. And then, you're in control. So maybe we could take more time—"

"I'll talk where and when I want to talk," Lena tells him.

She sounds like Rachael, he thinks.

"That's not really fair," he says, trying to keep his cool. "I mean, I told you everything about my life. Like, you're technically in my head right now—"

"I don't want to talk about this anymore," Lena says, turning away.

That one breaks him. He's tried so hard to be fair, and take it easy, and play by her rules. But being ignored, having his concerns swept away like they're dust, smashes right into him.

It's not right, and it's not fair. She's like everyone else, expecting him to play by her rules.

The ache deep within him hardens.

He's done. Done with this.

"Wow, great, then forget it," he says, throwing his hands in the air. "In my dreams, my only friend tells me to shut up when she feels like it, and in my real life, I get Lena the freaking Zombie. Sorry I even tried with you."

He can see the words hit her. Her facial expression gets struck down first, then her posture; she hugs her arms around her chest as the corners of her mouth pull down hard. It's the first time, he realizes, that Lena in her dreams has ever looked like the Lena he knows in the real world.

He's almost sorry he said it. But inside, he's still bristling.

"Get out," she says.

"You're in MY dreams!" he snaps. "YOU get out!"

"You want your dreams back?" she mutters, glowering at him. "Here you go."

Around them, the Mesa bursts into flames. Fires roar up out of the rocks in huge explosions, filling the air with searing heat and whipping smoke.

A storm cloud forms overhead, dark and churning, and out of it cracks a lightning bolt that fills the air with blinding light as it strikes between Simon and Lena. The rock floor of the Mesa opens up in a blackened crater, belching more flames and smoke.

Rachael rises out of the middle of the hole in the

ground, looking like some horrible ancient fire goddess. Her hair dances in the air like snakes, and though the flames surrounding her body roar, Simon can hear her cackling over it all. Behind her stands Lena, still staring daggers at him.

"That the best you've got?" he yells at Lena over Rachael's laughter and the whipping flames. "My sister? Come on, what'd you show the Franklin twins? What'd you show your brother?"

Lena's face twists in sadness and hatred. "Never talk to me again."

Rachael extends her hand, and Simon bursts into flames.

He sat up with a gasp and freed himself from the snarl of his blankets. He panted, trying to shake off the feeling of fire cascading around him, of his hair burning and his skin melting.

But mostly, he thought of that last look on Lena's face. The way he could tell he was ripping her heart out. How angry he was, how he kept going, kept pushing her.

Simon curled up in a ball, shaking and wishing dawn would come.

13

NIGHTMARE

"Well, this looks nice," said Mom as they piled out of
the car the next day.

Old Town Albuquerque was somewhere between
a village square and a preserved chunk of the Wild
West, its white adobe buildings dotted with protrud-
ing rafters and hung with signs advertising turquoise
jewelry, artisanal ice cream, and craft beer. At the center
of it all sat a park, a rare patch of green in the dusty
reddish-brown town, with a white gazebo at its center. The stretch of grass was packed with stalls and

vendors selling food, trinkets, woven goods, and colorful blown glass. By the gazebo, a band played, strumming acoustic guitars and beating on bongos. Off to one side, a man twisted a crank attached to a huge canister full of green chili peppers, which crackled as they spun over the open flame.

Simon flinched at the sight of the fire, the sound of the burning peppers.

It had been a long night.

He felt like he was experiencing the street fair through a hot, wet pillow. His body sagged and ached from sleeping so poorly, while the sun felt like a spotlight aimed directly at him, burning his eyes and skin. But maybe worse was how he felt inside, confused and tangled up. Every so often, he caught himself muttering about what an idiot he was, how stupid this had all been, how he might as well find the deepest, darkest cave in Albuquerque and crawl to its bottom.

"My dude, you okay?" asked Dad, rubbing Simon's shoulder.

"Yeah," said Simon, forcing a smile. "Just a little bright and loud."

"It's the altitude," said Dad, proudly spouting the Dad Fact he'd said a million times since they'd first gotten here. "The air is so thin that photons move through it easier than they do normal air."

"They know, Derek," said Mom. As always, her focus was on Aly, her fellow middle child. "What about you, Aly? Anything you want to do today?"

"Hmm? Oh, uh, no, nothing particularly." At least Simon wasn't alone in feeling weird. Aly was as agitated as ever, eyes darting back and forth, shoulders hunched, one wrist gripped firmly in her other hand. She kept taking these deep breaths that made her entire body heave, as though she was preparing herself for doing something drastic and difficult by going to the street fair. Simon guessed this was the most time she'd spent outside since they moved. It bothered him, sometimes, that he couldn't read her cloud and know what she was feeling. Then again, maybe that was for the best. Aly was having a tough time, and at least this way they were on equal footing.

They meandered through the stalls, Mom and Dad stopping to admire turquoise trinkets and buy a big bag of homemade tortilla chips. To Simon, the whole thing was like life with poor resolution. The colors and designs all felt dull and clumsy, nothing like the livid, vibrant world he'd been living in at night.

That was all in your head, he told himself. *Those are YOUR memories. Because you're not allowed to see hers. She didn't think you were good enough to let in.*

It didn't help, no matter how many times he told himself.

"All right, what should we check out next, gang?" asked Dad.

Simon looked up to answer—and noticed that Aly's eyes were pinned on him.

"I think Simon and I are going to walk around a little bit, if that's cool," she said. She looked at Dad and smiled tightly. "I have my phone. Meet you at the gazebo in, like, half an hour?"

Mom and Dad shared a glance, then cautiously nodded.

"All right, but don't eat a ton of snacks or any-thing," said Mom, handing Aly twenty dollars.

Aly steered them back between the stalls, and they walked side by side among the noise and the crowds. She stopped at a taco stand and got an orange soda, and they passed it between them silently.

"How're things going, dude?" she asked. "You okay? Seems like you've either been flying high or down in the dumps lately."

Simon shrugged and looked away. Classic Aly, thinking she had to make everything better. He liked it more when they were both quiet.

"Like you care," he said.

"I *do* care. That's why I'm asking. Checking in."

"Come on." Simon's feelings surged forward. "If it's not about trying to escape Rachael, it doesn't matter to you how I feel."

"We don't always have time to worry about how we *feel*," said Aly blankly.

Simon couldn't believe it. "Wow, okay."

"Simon, please for just one second think about—"

He rolled his eyes and booked it through the street fair, cutting between the stalls and down a side street. He was done with this, with Aly's long, empty explanations and the whole heartless mess his life had become. He walked forward hard, his shoulders and head down, until Aly ran up from behind him and blocked his path.

"Hey!" she said, moving next to him. "I'm sorry. I'm sorry if I made you feel like I only care about Rachael."

"It doesn't matter," he said, suddenly feeling even worse now that Aly had apologized. "Life just sucks, you know?"

"Sucks how?" asked Aly.

"I feel like I keep trying to be somebody I'm not," Simon told her, doing his best to put it into words. It was tough, but he was sick of dancing around how he really felt. How he'd felt all along. "This normal, helpful, fun kid. But you and Lena and everyone else keep thinking I'm a waste of time. Like I'm nice to have around, but I'm not really worth the effort."

"Lena—that's your friend, right?"

"See? You don't even know." Simon shook his head. "Why even bother if no one cares?"

"We care, I promise you." Aly stepped up to him and put her hands on his shoulders. "I'm sorry, Simon. I know this has been hard on you. We're all just adjusting in our own way. This is a new town for all of us. But!" she added as he shook his head again. "That doesn't mean we shouldn't be here for each other. And I'm really sorry if we made you feel left behind. I swear, I'll try harder. Just give me time, okay?"

Simon crossed his arms. He wanted to be stubborn, to push back, but this was a different sort of feeling that he'd had lately. He could hear the old Aly in his sister's voice, Aly who talked him out of his blank moments and treated him like an equal. Maybe that person was still inside the fortress.

"Fine," he said. "Fine, just . . . I'm so sick of feeling alone."

"You're not alone," Aly assured him. "You are many things, but you are not alone. *We* are not alone. We always have each other, even when Rachael's gone. Okay?"

"Okay," said Simon.

Aly hugged him, and Simon closed his eyes and let himself be held. It had been too long. It felt good to let go.

Maybe it would be all right.

Even with Rachael out there somewhere.

"Want to wander around the shops on the other side of this thing?" asked Aly. "I feel like these stalls are all really touristy."

"Sure."

"Okay, great," said Aly. "One sec, let me tie my shoe. Then we'll go." Aly bent over, and Simon's eyes scanned the hanging wooden signs. Pastries, a restaurant, a fancy-looking art gallery—

Cold, stinking liquid splashed across his face.

"BULLSEYE!" some guy yelled.

Aly staggered forward, her entire back splashed with the foul stuff. Simon wiped at his eyes, trying to make sense of what was happening, why he and his sister were covered with, by the overpowering smell of it, stale beer?

A crumpled beer can lay on the street between them, leaking foam.

Simon followed the sound of laughter to a pickup truck parked down the road. Three guys sat on the back bed of the truck with a cooler of beer cans between them. One of them, a lanky dude with a buzz cut wearing a Denver Broncos shirt, pumped his fist in the air. His friends hooted and cackled.

Simon couldn't believe it. His lips felt numb. Rage ballooned inside him like a mushroom cloud. Had this guy just *thrown a beer at them*?

"Okay, okay, be nice," said another guy, this dude with long hair and a thin mustache in a white *Rick and Morty* hoodie. He hopped off the truck bed and sauntered over to them.

"What the hell is wrong with you?" Aly yelled.

"I'm sorry, but you can't give Xavier a target like that and not expect him to toss one," said the long-haired boy. "Dude's team captain. There's an NFL career in his future."

"My arm's got a mind of its own!" shouted the dude in the truck.

Aly wasn't having it. "Sorry, is this what passes for a game in your mind? Have your friend throw a half-full beer at any girl who bends down to tie her shoelaces?"

"Come on," the long-haired guy said, rolling his eyes. "Calm down."

Simon forced the words through his rage-frozen lips. "Go away. Now."

The long-haired guy looked at him and cocked an eyebrow. "Bruh, nobody was talking to you. Get outta here before I teach you some manners."

Simon couldn't believe it. Even when he said what he felt, and there was a genuine moment where life wasn't a complete sewer, when he and Aly finally felt like family again, the world couldn't let it go. The universe itself had to splash beer all over his face to let him know that he was nothing, that trying to have something, to care about someone, to help people, none of that mattered. Because it wasn't meant for him. Nope. Not for Simon.

Simon closed his eyes. He opened his mind like a

hand, like the mouth of some giant Venus flytrap. He reached out and wrapped it around this guy's feeble little brain, a cloud of arrogance and anger and a million hormones in bloom.

In the palm of his mind, Simon could feel how small this guy's entire being was. How puny.

The thought hit him in a flash.

Rachael was right. She'd been right all along.

Simon's mind made a fist.

The guy's body twisted and seized, curving backward. Every muscle tensed, every tendon became a taut cord. His eyes rolled into their sockets, his hands clawed up next to his ribs, his lips yanked back revealing a checkered slab of gums and teeth. Foaming spit puffed out of the corners of his mouth, and he made a loud *EGH EGH EGH* noise as he tried to breathe.

"Taylor? Taylor!" The two guys hopped off the bed of the truck and ran toward their friend.

"SIMON, STOP!"

A burst of white.

Aly's palm connected with his face.

Simon stepped back, all of his anger taken out of him in a flash by Aly's slap. He saw the scene clearly for the first time—a guy on the ground mid-seizure, his friends screaming for help. People had broken away from the street fair, both tourists and vendors, but nobody could fully understand what they were seeing.

"Simon," said Aly, staring down at him, tears spilling over the edges of her wide eyes. "Simon, what have you done?"

"I'm sorry," he whispered. When he opened his mouth, he tasted hot copper, and realized that his nose was bleeding, gushing, creating a bib of crimson down his chin and the front of his shirt.

"You two! What happened here?" Aly and Simon looked up to see two cops in beige police uniforms jogging over. They looked around the scene in disbelief, trying to connect the dots and make sense of what they were witnessing.

"We don't know," said Aly. "He just started convulsing like that. I think he needs an ambulance."

"Ya think, kid?" said the cop. He yanked his radio to his mouth. "I need medical assistance over on Dora Northwest—"

The guys' pickup truck burst into flames.

There was a deafening roar.

A blast of heat.

Then . . . an explosion.

Aly and Simon fell to the ground, the heat slamming them in the face. Around them, everyone screamed and stampeded back to the fair.

Simon watched the flames lick up into the sky, sending a column of black, poisonous smoke into the air. He smelled burning rubber, and felt bits of upholstery fluff fall onto his arms and head.

He reached out with his mind. Felt through the panic of the crowds.

There. Somewhere behind them. A mind like an ember, bright and white-hot to the touch. Pleased with itself, excited to change the temperature in the room.

Rachael.

She'd found them.

14

WHAT DREAMS MAY COME

They'd barely stepped through the front door when Aly sprinted into the house. She'd been totally silent the entire ride home, and now she was alive, a cyclone of activity. A crash came from her room, and they jogged over to see what had happened.

In her room, Aly desperately unplugged her computer setup, tossing cables into a big pile in the center of the floor. Simon and Dad watched her, dumbfounded, uncomprehending, while Mom finally stepped in.

"Aly, honey, stop!"

"We need to go," panted Aly. "She's here, and she's coming for us, and we need to *go*."

"Aly, it was an accident," said Mom. She reached out for Aly, and Aly shrugged her off angrily. Mom grabbed her hard, spun her, and looked her in the eye. "Aly, listen to me! That wasn't Rachael! Rachael didn't blow up that car!"

"You don't know!" shrieked Aly, twisting against her grip. "You don't know what she can do!"

"Rachael isn't out there setting bombs, honey, okay?" said Mom, slow and loud. "You're feeling freaked out about what you saw, which is totally understandable. But you don't have to do this. We don't have to leave."

"Rachael can start fires with her mind," said Aly.

Simon gasped.

Boom. There it was.

Mom didn't want to hear it. "Aly, just stop."

"Rachael's pyrokinetic," shouted Aly. Her eyes flew to Simon. "Simon has powers, too. He can read people's minds, or auras or whatever. He can make their bodies move, like puppets. Simon, do it! Show them!"

Mom and Dad looked at Simon, and he bent inward, feeling like a turtle trying to suck back into his shell. He couldn't believe Aly had just outed them. After all the conversations they'd had, the almost-tellings, the playing-out of what would happen if they tried to have The Talk with their parents.

Now there it was. Their secret, out loud.

What if his parents were scared of him? What if the cops or the government found out, and tried to do tests on him and Rachael?

Simon shook his head at Aly. No. He couldn't. Not like this, in front of them.

"Simon, DO IT!" cried Aly, her eyes brimming with tears.

"You're scaring your brother, Aly," said Mom softly.

"No, but he—we need to get out of here—he knows—she's coming—she's—she's—we'll all—"

Aly began to pant faster and faster, her chest rising hard and quick, mouth open and teeth bared. She turned pale as her body began to shake all over. Mom realized what was happening, and pulled her in for a tight hug.

"Breathe, baby girl," she said softly. "You're having a panic attack. Just breathe, okay?"

"Aly?" asked Simon. "Aly!"

"Come on, my dude," said Dad, putting an arm across Simon's chest and pulling him out the door. "You don't need to see this."

Simon stared at the ceiling of his bedroom. He knew he had to do something, but he couldn't. He was wrung out, with all the energy and emotion squeezed from him in a blast of tragedy.

Using his powers to do that much harm—that was new. But it had come to him so effortlessly when that flash of world-shaking rage had hit him. Sure, his nose had bled like crazy, but the fact that he could just expand his power past its normal limits was unbelievable. He was as strong as ever.

It was almost cool.

But it was also really scary.

He hadn't been in control. Until Aly slapped him, his anger had taken the wheel.

That couldn't happen again.

Something had to change, he knew. It couldn't be like this. How long could his family last? How long before Aly had a nervous breakdown, or before his parents lost their minds about their family falling apart?

Before Rachael seriously hurt someone—maybe even killed them?

Rachael.

Simon shuddered to think of her so close. He'd thought so much about her feelings, who she was and whether he was like her, that he'd forgotten just how frightening it was to know that she was nearby.

Deep in his heart, he was glad Aly had warned their parents. He just wished she hadn't told them the rest of it.

He wanted to say he missed the normality of their life before, but they were never really normal. Rachael was always a drama queen, Aly was always killing herself trying to be helpful, and he was always helpless and terrified. But beneath all that, there was at least a feeling of love. Not like this, not nonstop fear and panic.

There was a way, he thought. Maybe, to save his family. To save some shred of what once was his life.

We're all gears, spinning, Aly had said, *and we're missing the one in the middle that connects us.*

He did the same thing he'd done earlier in the week—focused his power, thought of the words as though they had a mind of their own, and then poured urgency and fear into them, trying to give them the weight they deserved.

My sister is back, he thought. *She's coming for us. I need your help. Please.*

He closed his eyes and hoped that it would be enough as the day's fatigue dragged him down.

After today, the fireballs in Simon's dream are bigger. The heat sears him worse. The family's screams are bigger, their eyes wider, their faces are garish.

Simon is halfway across the kitchen when the fridge door swings open a crack.

His breath catches in his throat. He wades through the dream murk, pulls himself inside, and emerges onto the Mesa.

Lena waits for him in a long black coat over ripped jeans and a T-shirt with a glowing white circle on it. She watches Simon with a furrowed brow as he crosses the Mesa and approaches her. Seeing her leaves him feeling both frustrated and relieved; she's obviously not pleased to see him, but he has to admit that he likes being here, with her.

"Thank you," he says.

"I'm only here because my dad is one of the cops who was there today," she says. "He got a second-degree burn on his arm after the explosion."

"I'm so sorry," says Simon. "I didn't know your dad was a cop."

"Yeah, well . . . I didn't tell you." She stares off into the distance. "So, what can we do? I don't want my dad showing up to some burning building and dying in it because I let your sister run amok."

Simon gets right to the point. "Rachael's out there. Using my powers, I can feel her mind. We're going to go to her dreams."

"And what? Plant an idea?" asks Lena.

"No," says Simon. "We're going to track down where she is. And then I'm going to go find her myself."

15

BRING ME A DREAM

"What are we even looking for?" asks Lena as they join arms.

"I'm going to try to use my powers to feel around," he says. "I know her cloud really well. If she's close by, I'll find her."

"Feel around?" asks Lena, incredulous.

"I need to try this, Lena."

"Okay," she says, and takes a deep breath and closes her eyes. "Let's do it."

Simon reaches out to Lena and connects his mind

to hers. He's surprised by the flood of new emotions that seem to be shadowing the bottomless pit of her brain. Worry about her father. Guilt from watching her mom cry that night.

Frustration at Simon. Relief that she gets to see him again. Joy that they're here together.

"Okay," says Lena. "Here goes."

Once more, Simon lets the entire world shift around him as they rip through a sea of dreams, searching, listening to snippets of dialogue and echoes of screams. Simon silently hopes he isn't ruining the sleep of everyone in a five-block radius of his house as he pushes his cloud farther out, running the fingers of his mind through the churning landscape of everyone's subconsciouses, trying to grab a hard-to-describe feeling that he's only ever sensed in Rachael.

FIRE

There. He locks in on it, and pulls, drawing Lena and him to the dream.

A final gust of thoughts and voices, and they stand in a solid world. Both of them slowly open their eyes and blink back a barrage of loud colors.

"Are you sure this is her dream?" asks Lena.

"Definitely."

The mall around them is made entirely of light-blue plastic. All its stores are stocked with doll versions of expensive items—oversized gold watches, clunky smartphones with holographic stickers for screens, gaudy clothes made with frilly, glitter-caked cloth.

All around the floor wander people, their bobbling plastic heads wide-eyed and toothy, like poorly printed Barbies. The plastic-headed shoppers hustle clumsily and aimlessly among products, checking price tags and talking into their fake phones. They buy cheese-drenched food at the food court and chatter away about celebrity gossip and workout routines.

"Oh, I totally believe it, I totally believe it," squeals a nearby blond girl with a garish grin printed across her plastic face.

"There's no way, bruh," cackles a plastic-headed dude with a hoodie, sitting by a plastic fountain, its water frozen and highlighter blue. His friends cackle back, repeating his line—"No way, bruh, no way."

"What even is this place?" whispers Lena, watching the zombie-like shoppers wander past her.

"I think it's Rachael's dream." Simon's heart is pounding in his chest. Everything about this place makes him uncomfortable. Everyone's voices sound brittle and annoying. The colors are so bright that he feels like they are giving him a toothache.

He smells smoke.

One wall of the mall begins to bubble and blacken. The plastic heads all look up from their busybodying and stare at the burning structure.

The burning wall melts away in thick, sizzling globs.

In strides Rachael, a gray dress fluttering around her, her face set in a serene, content smile. She's exactly as Simon remembers her, only more confident, with her head held high and her expression exuding the kindness of a benevolent queen.

Behind her stalks a silhouette made entirely of flames. From its faceless head to the flickering tips of its feet, the shadow is composed of fire that shifts and flows, almost like water. The blazing human shape moves with Rachael, imitating her every gesture, and yet its movements are more fluid than hers, as though it follows her out of choice and not obligation.

Simon remembers something Aly had told him when she'd spoken to their Uncle Marco, who had also been a firestarter. Marco had told her, *The fire's a parasite.*

This, he realizes, is Rachael's fire.

As Rachael steps into the mall, she spreads her arms wide, and her fire-shadow does the same. All the plastic-head shoppers melt, their molded hair and painted-on eyes dripping and twisting horribly. Their skin bubbles, turns black, and eventually bursts into flames. Simon and Lena cower as the shoppers ignite one after another, fire flickering fast and loud across their bodies, until each one is made of embers and ashes, their burnt faces freed from their plastic masks. One after another, the charred people fall to their knees and hold up their hands, praying to Rachael.

Rachael reaches out to one of the kneeling ash-people. The burnt thing puts its hand in hers—but its fingers crumble into dust in her gentle grip. An expression of sadness crosses Rachael's face, but she simply sighs and moves on to the next kneeling figure.

"Oh God," whispers Simon, his stomach churning and his skin crawling. He'd thought his recurring dream was disturbing and he'd known there was something wrong with his sister, but THIS . . .

"Simon, look," says Lena, pointing.

Simon's eyes follow her finger. A trail of flaming black scars the ground where Rachael has walked, moving out of the opening in the wall and creating a perfect line across the countryside. At the end of it, Simon sees a large square building in the distance, looking dark and abandoned. There's a huge *M* and *D* printed on the side.

"What does it mean?" Simon asks.

Lena turns to answer him. But before she can, she glances over his shoulder and gasps. Her hand seizes his upper arm in panic.

When Simon turns, the fire is looking at him.

Rachael still walks from one devotee to another, but her fire-shadow has stopped, and has turned its blank, bulbous head toward them. This close, Simon can feel the heat coming off the creature's body. Though its face is only roiling flames, Simon can sense eyes somewhere behind the fire, watching him intently.

"Can it see us?" he whispers.

"No one's ever seen me before," Lena whispers back. She swallows hard. "But it's a dream. Anything is possible."

The fire-shadow stretches one of its long, wispy arms over to Rachael and gently strokes her shoulder. Rachael scowls, claps the ash off her hands, and looks over her shoulder.

Her eyes land on Simon's.

A smile grows on her face. The smile Simon knows, from his dream.

"Well, well, well!" laughs Rachael.

She extends a hand toward them.

The fire-shadow does the same, and out of it pours blue flame.

Lena darts in front of Simon and holds up her own hands. The fire never reaches them, billowing around them in a dome. She's blocking it, Simon realizes, using her powers to stop Rachael from burning them.

But by the look of her gritted teeth and clenched eyes, she's having a hard time.

Rachael laughs louder, her cackle filling the room, the sky, the entire world. She pushes her hands out farther, and the fire-shadow does the same.

The heat grows. The flames turn white, blinding them.

Lena screams.

Simon gasped and shot out of bed, his chest rising and falling. He realized, after a moment, that he must have been holding his breath. His pillow was soaked with sweat. A single line of blood ran out of his nose and down the side of his cheek.

Before he could fully understand what was happening, his phone buzzed next to his bed. He looked and saw an unknown number, but somehow knew it was Lena.

"Are you okay?" he whispered after answering.

On the other end, Lena was crying.

"I'm so sorry, Lena," he said. "I didn't know."

She sniffed hard, and then, after a moment, told him, "The building with the *M* and the *D*."

"What?"

"It's a warehouse around here," she whispered. "I know where it is."

16

FIREPLACE

He was lucky that Aly was taking today to rest up, Simon thought as he wolfed down an English muffin. Mom went about her morning as usual, too absorbed in grown-up worries to notice how jittery he was probably acting. But Aly was intuitive, and would've picked up on it immediately. She would've heard the quiver in Simon's voice when he said he was "spending Sunday at his new friend's house," and would've known something was up.

He climbed on his bike and took off out of the

130

driveway. A few minutes of confusing directions later, he wheeled into a suburban neighborhood, past rows and rows of squat adobe houses, until he reached the white metal fence around the stone-filled lawn with cacti growing in small garden boxes outside. Among them were kids' toys—a plastic slide covered with clouds and stars, a fire truck with little Playskool firemen, and a mini-trampoline. From inside, he could hear a toddler shouting, accompanied by an adult trying to calmly talk her down.

Simon was past the gate and halfway up the front path when the door opened and a lanky guy came blasting out, yelling, "Yeah, I got it!" over his shoulder. He wore ripped-up jeans and a shirt with a band name on it in spiny letters. He had a spiked piercing jutting out of the center of his lower lip. When he saw Simon, he stopped and scowled.

"Who are you?" he asked.

"Uh, is Lena home?" Simon responded, feeling like the littlest kid in the world beneath the guy's stare.

The teenage guy rolled his eyes and called, "LENA, GUY HERE FOR YOU" over his shoulder. Then he brushed past Simon, hopped into a nearby parked car, and drove off, blasting furious metal as he shrieked around a corner.

Before Simon knew what was happening, Lena came out. She said nothing but "Come on," then led him to the garage where she grabbed her own bike.

"Was that your brother?" asked Simon as they turned off into the street.

Lena nodded hard, but stared straight ahead. "This way," she said.

Simon took her lead, and the two rode out of her small suburban neighborhood and through Downtown, with its hipstery coffee shops and venues. Around them, people were just starting up their day, walking to work with coffees and spinning window signs from CLOSED to OPEN. Simon watched them living their normal lives, and lightly reached out with his mind. All he felt in their various clouds were minor worries—cares about money, memories of TV they'd watched last night. He wondered how they'd feel if they knew that people like him, Lena, and Rachael were out there among them, peering into dreams, playing with their minds, or setting their cars on fire.

Downtown fell away, and they were in an industrial complex, with fortress-sized buildings spread out across huge strip-mall lots between backstreets. Soon, company and store logos left the buildings' sides, and the warehouses and storage units were entirely blank, their gray and blue walls as faceless and silent as the mountains in the distance.

"There," said Lena, veering her bike toward one old building.

The warehouse looked totally abandoned. Its windows were boarded up and a lone tire lay on its side in the parking lot. It looked like every other warehouse Simon had ever seen, and he wondered how Lena knew this was the one.

His eyes scanned the huge letters along the side.

NEW   EXICO LUMBER   EPOT

Missing an *M* and a *D*. The letters that had been on the side of the building in Rachael's dream.

It had to be.

They pulled around to the side of the building and ditched their bikes near the service entrance. Simon noticed security cameras along doorways and window-sills, but none of them showed any signs of lighting up or moving to follow them.

He and Lena walked the perimeter of the ware-house, seeing nothing but litter and sand . . . until they came across a boarded-up door where the plywood was set aside just a bit.

Its edges had been burned.

"Here we go," said Simon. He pressed on the plywood, and it moved. Slowly, he and Lena pushed it aside, ducking into the darkness of the warehouse.

If the outside of the place looked abandoned, the inside proved it was. The warehouse was a shadowy expanse of corridors, visible via dim shafts of daylight coming in from the windows that only seemed to make the room's dark corners even darker. Stacks of old boxes lined the floor, many of them rotting and crumbling to reveal faded paperwork and newspapers. The room swallowed up all sound, except for the occasional tap-tapping and shuffling of vermin crawling out of their way.

Looking down at the floor, Simon saw a handful of tiny red markings scuttling away into the darkness. Black widows. They were everywhere in Albuquerque.

He and Lena walked silently through the warehouse, scanning the dark rows. Finally, Simon's eyes found the shape of a door outlined in light against the far wall.

"There," he whispered.

They crept to the doorway, which up close was painted the same soup-yellow color as the walls. It had a sign marked EMPLOYEES ONLY taped to it. Simon curled his fingers around the edge of the door, put his eye to the crack, and gently pulled it open.

He heard middle-aged women. Arguing. Loudly.

What had obviously been an employee lounge—a kitchen station, couches facing a TV in one corner, a small table and chairs—had been turned into the polar opposite of the warehouse. Colorful shag blankets and tasseled throw pillows lined every surface. A collage of fashion magazine cutouts and band posters lined every square inch of wall space, except for an open section by the screen where someone had spraypainted *FTV* in six-foot-high letters. The table was piled with open bags of snacks and microwave dinner packaging, and the kitchen sink overflowed with dirty dishes and garbage. Pulsing LED strings and fairy lights dangled from nails sloppily punched into the ceiling, and gave the room a bizarre nightclub vibe.

Unlike the rest of the warehouse, Simon noted, everything in here was new, and pretty expensive-looking. A huge TV sat in the corner, its massive

HD screen alive with reality-show Real Housewives screaming about whose dinner party was more expensive.

"Which Real Housewife of Hoboken do you think would win in a real fight, Andrea or Lisa?"

Simon stiffened.

That was Rachael's voice.

But from where?

"I'm voting Lisa," was a boy's nasal reply. "She got them big biceps. Alligator arms. You know those come into play when she hulks out."

"Word."

Wait, was she—

Simon pulled the door open a little farther.

Its hinges creaked like a screaming cat.

Rachael's head popped up over the back of the couch, where she'd been lying down. Her eyes locked with Simon's—and she grinned.

"Well, well, well!" she said.

Simon felt cold all over. Caught.

"Let's get out of here," he said.

He and Lena turned, but a girl he hadn't noticed blocked their path and grabbed his arm. She was willowy and pale, with big, unblinking eyes and long blond hair hanging wetly down one side of her face. In her free hand were a towel and a toothbrush.

"Hey, wait," she said.

Simon tried to twist out of her grasp.

The girl wouldn't let go.

"Get out of my way," said Simon.

"Make me," the girl replied.

Simon's panic turned to frustration and anger.

"Have it your way," he said.

He reached out with his mind, grabbed, and pushed.

The girl grabbed back, and pulled.

Simon felt his body stiffen as the girl sucked him into her gaze, her eye, the endless pool of her pupils, until everything around him was total blackness. He felt as though he was having the wind knocked out of every part of his body, and then all at once he was plummeting, falling through ice-cold darkness forever, with nothing to save him.

17

DREAM TEAM

"Easy! Easy!"

Simon gasped as the world swam back into view. He was on his knees, trembling, cold with sweat. Lena shook him by the shoulders, her face tight with concern. Rachael stood between him and the icy-looking blond girl, who backed slowly away but never took her glazed stare off Simon.

"Maybe go half that hard next time, okay, Joyce?" said Rachael.

"*Sorry*," cooed the blond unapologetically.

"It's fine, just, c'mon, he's only a kid." Rachael turned and crouched to face him. Simon's memories of his sister were always of her in the grips of her growth spurt, wearing bright colors and tons of makeup, just like she had when she'd first started using her powers. But here she was, in a white shirt and jeans, smiling at him with an ease he'd never seen on her before. He couldn't help but remember his thoughts from the street fair—*Rachael was right*. That's how his sister looked now: like she knew she was right. Like she knew she'd been right all along.

"What *was* that?" he asked weakly, trying to regain his bearings and figure out exactly what was going on.

"That's Joyce's power," Rachael answered, hiking a thumb back at the other girl. She put a hand under Simon's arm and helped pull him to his feet. "She's like a black hole. And if you try to use your power on her, she can, like, grab it and drain you. This is only the second time I've seen her use it. First time was on me, so I know what you're feeling."

A sliver of the cold emptiness he'd just experienced flashed across Simon's senses, and he shuddered. *A black hole.*

The skinny blond girl was terrifying.

"What are you going to do to us?" asked Simon. He stepped away from Rachael and shook his arms and legs, trying to get some feeling back in them. "Keep in mind that my phone tracker is on, so Mom knows where I am."

"Actually, she doesn't." From the couch, a boy in black skinny jeans and a shirt reading DETHKLOK waved at Simon. He had a big round face with a snarky smile, each cheek a lasagna of acne. "I've redirected the tracker signal to one of those GPS dog collars. If she's looking for you, she's gonna see you playing fetch in a front yard two towns away."

"Colin, that's *genius*," said Rachael. She grinned at Simon. "How cool is *that*? Colin's a *technopath*!"

"Cyberpath!" Colin called out.

"Yeah, whatever," said Rachael. "He's, like, a psychic hacker. He can infiltrate any phone or computer with his brain. It's *mind-blowing* that he exists, right? Makes you think there's, like, a zoo's worth of people out there like us."

"Where'd you find these people?" Simon asked, trying to wrap his head around the idea of someone using these kinds of powers to go online.

"They found me, actually," she said. "They'd heard about my story, and were looking for people like them. Like *us*." She smirked at him. "But I guess you found me, too, huh? I should've known you'd be here after last night. I assume your lady friend can do dream stuff? She seemed pretty good at it then."

Simon looked at Lena, who hugged herself silently. She met his eyes and gave him a slight shake of her head, but he got the message. *I don't like this at all.*

Simon's gaze moved back and forth between the three teenagers. Colin smirked, but his eyes darted quickly between the others, while Joyce sat motionless on the kitchen counter, staring at the floor. Classic Rachael, surrounding herself with a crew of people who were too quiet and introverted to speak over her. Like him and Aly, only sadder. At least he and Aly were related to her. They *had* to know her.

"Rachael," he said, taking a deep breath, "I want to ask you to come home."

"Mmmno," said Rachael.

"Rachael . . . this has gotta stop," Simon pleaded. He relived the dream behind his eyes. Her face in the doorway, the overpowering heat on his cheeks. "I came here because I'm sick of waking up every night,

scared of being burned to death. Our family is terrified of you. *Please*—"

"Whoa, hey, what am I hearing?" Rachael cocked an
eyebrow and held up her palms. "First of all, *I* didn't leave
our family in a hospital and then move away when they
woke up. Second, I'm not trying to burn anyone alive. I
mean, honestly, Simon, if I'd wanted to hurt you or your
friend here"—she snapped her fingers, and a fireball
erupted from her hand—"I could have." She frowned,
looking hurt. "Is that really why you came here? Because
you think I'm planning to torch you? *Boo!*"

"You burned down our home," he said. "And you
burned down our house in Texas, too."

"Yeah, but I was super angry then," she said,
crossing her arms. "I'd just lost two months in a hospital because you scrambled my brain, remember?
Honestly, *I'm* the one who should be scared of *you*,
Simon. You're *way* more powerful than me."

"Then why did you follow us?" he asked. "Is this
another master plan? Are you going to pin your crimes
on me, like you tried to pin them on Aly?"

"Okay, so, master plan *yes*, frame-up *no*. Before
you say anything else, let me ask you this: How'd it feel
putting that creep at the street fair in the hospital?"

Simon said nothing.

But Rachael saw his answer on his face.

"Exactly," she said. "We all know those dudes deserved it. What else could you do, Simon? They all but assaulted Aly. You did *exactly* what you had to do."

Simon bit the inside of his cheek.

He hated how proud he felt, hearing that.

"You did good, Simon," said Rachael. "You knew what the right thing to do was, and you did it, because you could. There's a name for that kind of behavior: heroism. And that's the kind of behavior this crew needs."

Lena snorted and shook her head. "She's kidding, right?" she mumbled. "*Superheroes.* We're really doing *that*."

"No, no, no," said Rachael quickly, like she'd been ready for that reaction. "No costumes, no CGI-choked sequel of a sequel. But! What I'm talking about is no longer living like chumps. Taking what we want, having what we want, and helping people along the way."

"If we can," mumbled Joyce.

"If we can," echoed Rachael. "Basically be the people everyone else wants to be. FTV"—she pointed at the tag on the wall—"that's our name right now. Fire Tech Void. Cool, right? For now, it's grassroots, though eventually, I'm thinking we might *want* to go public with it? Make it kind of a personal brand? I figure we launch an Instagram and TikTok and go from there. Though maybe neither of those—that sounds gross the minute I say it. There'll probably be a new platform by then. I refuse to do Meta, though. VR goggles? Come on, what kind of bad '80s movie—"

"Rachael!" said Simon.

"Right, sorry, okay, point is, you're a good guy with an incredible heart and one of the most powerful brains in the world. So why are you eating school lunches? In *Albuquerque*? Why are we not showing the world that we're not to be messed with?"

"I'm just some kid, Rachael," said Simon. "I just turned eleven. I'm not—"

Rachael held up her right hand, and it burst into flames.

Simon and Lena stepped back, shielding their faces from the heat. Rachael looked at her arm as fire coursed over it in rippling waves. And yet, Simon noticed, though they roared off her hand and seared his eyebrows, the flames never burned her. Not a hair on her arm blackened. She was in total control.

"And this is *all* I can do," she said. "Fire is cool

to look at, but Simon, you're *in people's heads*! Don't buy the just-kids baloney that Aly and people like her want to feed you. You were made better than normal people. Why not *own the world*?"

"So it's super*villains*," said Lena softly. "Worse."

Rachael looked over at Lena. Simon watched a flash of dead-eyed hatred cross his sister's face, as though the fire was thinking for her. Then she snapped her fingers, the flames shut off, and she burst into laughter. Across the room, Colin joined in with a snicker.

"Babe, does your power even work while you're awake?" Rachael asked.

Lena was silent.

"Right." Rachael shot Simon an embarrassed look. "So you have to *be asleep* to do anything? And then you, what . . . influence people? *Please*. Maybe when we're forty and, like, need to convince a mayor to pass a proposition or something, we'll call you. Right now, I'm looking for champions, not dreamgirls."

Lena shook her head. "I've seen your dreams."

"So?" said Rachael.

"So this will crumble, too," said Lena.

Rachael's smile didn't deflate entirely. But Simon watched it lose a lot of its steam.

"*AN*Yway," she said, turning back to Simon, "I'm not going to force you to do anything, dude. I'm just saying that, if I'm reading things right, you've realized life isn't fair. Which, hey, congrats. But evolution gave you an ace up your sleeve. And *I'm* saying that maybe you should play that ace to its fullest extent. Hang with us."

The idea rolled over in Simon's mind. Rachael's words had hit him hard, made him realize that she knew what he was going through more than anyone else, more than Aly, Mom, or even Lena. All his recent feelings of not wanting to be helpless anymore—Rachael not only understood them, but she'd done something about them. One day, she'd woken up special but hating her life, and she'd used her abilities to do what she felt like. Aly could play the *just another kid* card all she wanted, but it was Rachael who knew what it was like to feel underappreciated, and scared . . .

. . . to escape a burning house . . .

"What's the good life?" asked Simon. "Ice cream sundaes every night, all the YouTube you want?"

"Sure, if that's your thing!" said Rachael, perking up. "Sounds fun, right?"

"Living in abandoned buildings?" he continued.

"Dodging black widows when you come back from the bathroom? Never seeing your family? Running from the police, and who knows who else?"

Rachael huffed. "Oh, you're not actually excited. You're ripping on me. *Booooo!*"

"Yeah, boo," he said, feeling outrage rise in him. He stepped toward her, balling his fists at his sides. "Rachael, you're my sister, and I love you. And you're right, life sucked a *lot* when I was some helpless kid. But it sucks a lot more since you sent us on the run. Do you know that Aly had a panic attack when she realized you were here?"

"Of course she did," Rachael sighed. "She's so dramatic, right?"

"Rachael, you're not listening to me," he said. "It's been a year and a half. I'm so tired. And I'm not interested in letting you ruin my life anymore by making me part of your scary gang. Either come home and be a part of our family again, or just leave us alone."

Rachael sighed. Simon could swear he saw her exhale a little smoke.

"I'm going to give you time to think this over," she said. "We'll talk soon."

"It'll be 'no' then, too," said Simon. "Come on, Lena."

He took Lena's hand and led her past Rachael. Joyce stood and went to block their way, but Rachael called out, "No, it's okay. Let them go."

Simon and Lena didn't say a word to each other as they left. It didn't feel safe. As they picked up their bikes outside, Rachael came to the door and watched them go.

"Say hi to Mom and Dad for me!" she called out.

18

NIGHT PEOPLE

Simon and Lena stopped at a gas station a few blocks away to catch their breaths and talk about what to do next. Lena was visibly intimidated by the encounter; Simon watched her hands shake as she sipped the Dr Pepper he'd bought them.

"She's not going to hurt us," Simon assured her.

"How do you know?" asked Lena.

"I . . . just know," said Simon. He couldn't really explain it—he hadn't even used his powers to read Rachael's feelings or intentions. But he'd known his oldest sister his entire life, and he could hear when she was truly furious, or feeling divisive. When she'd lied to Aly and set her up, Simon had suspected something from her tone of voice alone. That wasn't how Rachael had behaved back in that warehouse. She was playing a different game.

Lena sneered, unconvinced. "So do we just wait until she blows something else up?" she asked. "She hurt my dad, Simon. She's dangerous."

"You're right," he said. "We need to keep her from causing any more trouble. The question is . . . how?"

"What about your other sister? Could she help?"

"No," said Simon, too fast. The image of Aly convulsing with shallow breaths echoed through his mind. "She's too stressed already. If she finds out about this, she'll spend all night drawing up blueprints and drinking Red Bull. It'll give her another panic attack."

Lena scowled. "So your sister's health matters. But my dad's doesn't."

"That's not what I'm saying," said Simon, but he felt guilty denying it. Yeah, Rachael was a danger to the people around her. But, as much as he hated to admit it, he had liked seeing her. As Aly had mentioned, he missed her, even if he didn't want to.

And, he had to admit, there was a part of him that liked what she had to say.

Everyone else was telling him to keep his powers a secret, be gentle with the people around him, live according to what *they* thought was right, what *they* wanted from Simon. Rachael was the first person to acknowledge how strong he was. Rachael made him want to say, out loud, *I'm powerful. I can do whatever I want.*

Lena's phone beeped. She glanced at it and stood. "My mom. I gotta go."

Simon heaved a sigh, worried he'd somehow offended her. But after climbing on her bike, she looked over her shoulder at him.

"Can we talk more about this tonight?" she asked.

"I'd really like that," he said.

"Good," she said. She smiled at him—a small smile, but it was there—and then rode off.

The rest of the day was spent getting ready for bed. Simon did his homework and ate dinner in a haze, wondering what to do with Rachael. Over and over, he replayed their interaction and got stuck on her words.

You did good, Simon.

There's a name for that kind of behavior: heroism.

He forced the thoughts out of his mind. He couldn't just run off with Rachael. He had to be bigger than that—for Aly. For Lena.

He must have seemed out of it, because after dinner, Mom kept asking him if everything was okay. He mumbled some responses, but inside, he was dying. He wanted desperately to reveal that Rachael was just a few minutes' car ride away, to let her know that Aly had been telling the truth and that they were in grave danger.

But he knew how that would unfold. Mom would call the cops. The cops would shoulder their way in, thinking they were dealing with a couple of scabby runaway kids.

The building would burn. People would get hurt, maybe die.

He swallowed down the urge to tell her. No doubt Rachael knew he would. He'd done his best to get in her face, but she knew exactly how scary she was.

At bedtime, he lay awake in his dark room, wondering what he should do. He knew that Lena was waiting for him on the other side of the fridge, ready to talk out their plans. But he felt conflicted. Almost embarrassed.

What if this time, he didn't dream about their house burning down? What if he dreamed about him and Rachael walking the earth like giants, taking over the world—

Tap tap tap.

Simon sat up. What was that?

"Psst! Simon, open up!"

Someone was at his window.

Simon crept out of bed and pulled up the blinds.

Rachael grinned and waved at him from the other side.

Simon gasped. What was this? Slowly, doing his best to stay quiet, he opened the window. Rachael stood in their backyard with Colin and Joyce a few feet back.

"What are you doing here?" hissed Simon.

"I felt bad about how we left things," she said. "I figure I should show you what we mean. Come out with us. We're going to party."

"Do you want Mom and Dad to see you? This is a smart house. It has all these security cameras—"

"Colin's handling it," Rachael said coldly. "See? What *can't* we do? Anyway, come out and rage. I promise we'll have a good time."

"Rachael, I can't just climb out a window and hang out with you!"

Rachael looked around, confused. "Why not? Who's stopping you?"

Simon tried to find a good answer for that. *You're a wanted criminal. Aly would be so angry. I have plans.*

"I have to meet my friend," he said. "In . . ."

"In your dreams? Really? You're blowing me off to *sleep*?"

"She's—"

"Simon, you can do the stuff people dream about," Rachael said, flopping her arms down at her sides, "and you're gonna spend your night *talking to someone* in your *dreams*?"

When she put it that way . . .

He knew he shouldn't do it. He knew he should stay home and talk to Lena. Rachael was out of control, and her friends weirded him out.

He shouldn't want to go out. He should . . .

"Let me get dressed," he said. "Where are we going?"

Rachael's face lit up. "Great! Bring your swim trunks, if you have them."

"Swim trunks?"

"You'll see."

19

LIVING THE DREAM

Cool.

Simon realized he'd never known what that felt like before now.

But as he climbed off the bus and walked alongside Rachael and her friends, the city lit up neon and sparkling around him, he felt cool for the first time. He walked slowly, his head up high, his shoulders wide, his gaze level. He didn't avoid eye contact with strangers, or worry about what people might think of him. It was like Rachael's overpowering confidence was contagious. Next to her, he felt like he could do whatever he wanted.

Because, he quickly realized, he could.

"Check it," said Rachael. She nodded toward a heavyset man in a leather jacket lighting a huge cigar. Rachael winked at him, and suddenly the flame from his lighter was five feet tall and curved into the form of a smiley face. The man stumbled back, while onlookers pointed and gasped.

"My turn," said Colin. He pointed at a theater up ahead where a big digital marquee promised an upcoming concert. Colin put a finger to his temple, squinted—and then the marquee flickered, and read FTV in huge blinking letters.

"YES!" said Rachael, throwing a fist in the air. "Colin, you're brilliant."

"If you've got it, flaunt it," he said. "Simon, you do one."

Simon stumbled a bit, his sudden sense of coolness momentarily shaken. "Sorry?"

"Do one," said Colin. "Show us what you got!"

"Uh . . ." Simon tensed up. Just use his powers? For a gag, in public, on some random stranger? School was one thing—there, he'd helped people—but this could be catastrophic. What if he accidentally hurt someone? What if—

"You don't have to if you don't want to," said Rachael. She shot him a smile he'd seen a million times on Mom and Aly. Reassuring, letting him know that she understood. That no one expected much from a little boy like him.

That he was *the baby*.

Simon looked out at the crowds in the streets. A few yards away, at a restaurant's patio, a man raised a burrito to his lips.

Simon reached out into the cloud of his mind, grabbed, and twisted.

In an instant, the man tossed his burrito ten feet into the air. It plummeted back toward his plate— where he caught it with an astounded expression.

Rachael guffawed. Colin clapped, shaking his head.

"I can't believe you just *did that*!" Rachael chuckled. "The throw was cool, but that *catch*? Oh my God, you're incredible, dude!"

"I try," Simon said with a smile. He glanced down past Rachael and Colin, to where Joyce silently walked alongside them. "Is . . . is Joyce going to do one now?"

"NO," said Rachael and Colin at the same time, and then they burst into laughter once more. Joyce smiled, just a little, but stayed quiet.

"Here it is," said Colin, pointing ahead of them. A huge, luxurious hotel sat two blocks away, a valet standing dutifully beneath its front awning. Colin marched forward toward the door, while Rachael held out a hand to stop Simon from following him.

"Colin's going to figure out our reservation," said Rachael. When she saw the confusion on Simon's face, she smiled again. "That's his strong suit, honestly. If you control technology these days, it means you control money. He can make credit card accounts appear and disappear."

Simon shook his head at the idea of it. No money, no rules. It couldn't be real, could it?

"Here we go," said Colin, jogging back over with a set of key cards in his hand. "We're booked for the night. The Southwest Royalty suite."

"That's what I'm talking about," said Rachael. "And is that the one . . . ?"

"Yes, yes," said Colin, nodding. He shot an eye roll at Simon. "I'm sure you know this already, man, but your sister has elaborate tastes."

*   *   *

Simon licked grease and ketchup from his lips.

"What's the verdict?" Rachael asked.

He smiled. "Best burger I've ever eaten. In a hot tub. In a hotel room."

Rachael threw her head back and howled in laughter. She, Simon, and Colin all floated in a hot tub in the middle of a hotel suite living room, with the sprawl of Downtown Albuquerque glittering outside its windows.

Simon couldn't really believe it was happening, and kept wondering if maybe he had fallen asleep and this was a dream he was having. But, he reasoned, if he was sleeping, Lena would've shown up by now. Instead, he was actually living like a rock star. The massive bacon cheeseburger in his hands was delicious. *Thor: Love and Thunder* blasted on a wall-sized screen behind him. A room service cart piled high with milkshakes and fried appetizers sat by the door.

And Rachael, he realized, had just made it happen. She and her friends had used their powers however they wanted, and then, bam, they were having so much fun that Simon questioned whether or not he was actually awake.

"Why do you live in a warehouse if you can just

159

make a hotel reservation using your brain at any time?" he asked, enjoying the water jet against his lower back.

"Oh, we never stay the night," said Colin through a mouthful of mozzarella sticks.

"Joyce taught us that," Rachael added. "The morning shifts at the hotels are always ready to look a little closer at guests and their reservations. If you leave before sunrise, though, most people don't even notice. The warehouse is just a crash pad. It's nice, except that the bathroom's all the way across the freakin' building!"

Simon laughed along with Colin. He had tried not to be impressed with his sister's new way of living, but so far, it seemed pretty awesome. When he'd previously imagined her going from city to city following them, he'd always pictured her hitchhiking or eating out of dumpsters. Instead, her life rivaled that of any celebrity's.

"But this is nice, huh?" she asked, lightly kicking Simon's thigh. "Having all the stuff you've ever dreamed of? And who gets hurt? A big hotel chain, with billions of dollars that it probably doesn't even pay its workers?"

Simon smiled and shrugged. "Hot tub cheeseburger is not a bad way to live."

"Truth," said Rachael. "That's something else Joyce really got me to thinking—that there's nothing people like us can't have." She smiled and squeezed Simon's shoulder. "And that once we're all together, we're going to be unstoppable."

"Hey, where is Joyce, anyway?" asked Colin. "I feel like she disappeared the minute she got here."

"Yeah, she's been quiet lately," said Rachael. "Or quiet-*er*. I can go check on her."

"It's fine, I'll look around for her," said Simon, rising from the Jacuzzi. "I have to pee, anyway."

"Shoulda just peed in the tub!" yelled Rachael. "It's what I'm doing!" Colin and Simon shared a disgusted look and gagging noise, and then Simon walked dripping toward the bathroom. He took a weird pleasure in not drying off his bathing suit immediately, trailing hot tub water all across the suite. Not his tub, not his problem. He'd be out of there by morning.

Out of here by morning.

For the first time, he let himself entertain the thought.

What if he left?

What if he joined up with Rachael and her friends? Hopped a bus or a train, headed out into the world.

California, New York, wherever people go to start over. Use his powers to help people along the way and live like a king otherwise. What was he really missing? School? Who cared about geometry or Greek gods?

Mom, Dad, and Aly. That would be rough. But the past couple of months had just wiped him out, and so often he felt like a pain in his family's neck. And if he left with Rachael, then there was no fear of Rachael coming after them. His family wouldn't have to fear for their lives any longer.

Lena. But sometimes he wondered if Lena kind of hated him now. And anyway, all he'd caused her was drama since he'd shown up. Maybe she deserved a life without him.

Would they be better off without him?

Would he, would *everyone*, be happier if he left?

He was so lost in thought that he burst into the bathroom without knocking.

Joyce was hunched over the sink, her hair dangling in her face. She heaved and hacked, coughing harder and louder than anyone Simon had ever heard.

She spit, and a thick wad of blood hit the sink. Crimson droplets spattered out across the white countertop. The sight made Simon wince, but he couldn't look away.

"Whoa," he said.

Joyce looked up at him. Simon could see one of her eyes through the curtain of her hair, wide and angry. Her lips were smeared with blood, and drooled a long string of red down into the sink.

"What?" she whispered.

"Are you okay?" Simon asked.

"Fine," she replied.

"Uh . . . okay, well, everyone's just asking after you," he said, slowly backing out of the bathroom.

Uh-oh. Simon padded back to the hot tub, determined. Whatever was going on in there, Rachael had to know. What if they'd caught some sort of disease or gotten an infection while living in that warehouse? He wasn't trying to snitch on Joyce, but he didn't want to see his sister get some horrible virus and cough up a lung.

"Hey, guys," said Simon as he walked back into the living room—only now, the hot tub was empty.

Colin was pulling on his T-shirt. Rachael stood dripping at the door, talking to a skinny man in a suit with a frustrated look on his face. His gold name tag told Simon he worked for the hotel.

"There must be some misunderstanding," she said.

"I agree, miss," said the man, pointing to a tablet in his hand. "But until we figure out this payment issue, I must ask you and your friends to leave the room."

"Have you called my father?" asked Rachael. "He should be able to sort this all out."

"Unfortunately, the number you've given us appears to be out of service," said the hotel employee. "So until we can contact him, or unless you want him to reach out to us, I'm going to have to ask that you wait in the lobby."

"Yeesh, okay, let me change," said Rachael. She turned and closed the door—but the man put an arm out and held it open.

"*Actually*," said the man, "I'm happy to wait while you get changed in a bedroom. But I think it's best I stay here until you've all left."

Rachael stared blankly at the hotel employee. Once again, Simon saw the look she'd given Lena, that praying-mantis gaze that told him she had made a decision not to care about someone. Simon wondered if she was picturing the man's plastic head blackening and melting.

"Simon," she said, looking back at her brother. "Can you handle this?"

Simon cringed. Now? Here, to this random guy? What was Rachael expecting him to do, with that look on her face?

They were looking at him. He had to do *something*.

He reached out—carefully—and seized the man's mind. He felt his anger at these bratty kids, frustration at his own staff for not calling him when four teenagers checked in without an adult . . .

There.

Simon pulled.

The man jerked into a rigid standing position with a *HGK!* noise. He took a step back, grabbed the doorknob—and slammed the door in his own face. No scream, no alarm, just the sounds of his jerky footsteps moving down the hall.

Rachael clapped as Simon let the man go. "Yes. YES. See, Colin, this is what I'm talking about. This is why Simon's necessary for this team."

"It's pretty incredible, I gotta admit," said Colin.

He walked over and gave Simon a light punch on the shoulder. "Feels good, right?"

"Yeah, well, you're the one who got us the hotel," said Simon, laughing a little. He'd been so scared to use his powers, but here everyone was, applauding him. "So, what, you think he'll just leave us alone?"

"Oh, no, we definitely need to leave," said Rachael. "Come on, get dressed and grab whatever soap and towels you can carry."

They had just finished getting their clothes on when there were three loud bangs on the door.

"SECURITY. OPEN UP."

Rachael groaned. "Welp, we're doing this the hard way. Colin?"

"On it," said Colin. He had his fingers up against his temples, and his eyes darted back and forth quickly. *BANG BANG BANG.*

"What's the hard way?" asked Simon.

"Just stay close to me, and keep your head down until we're outside," said Rachael.

"SECURITY! OPEN THE DOOR!"

"Colin?" asked Rachael.

"Still looking for an empty one," said Colin.

"Joyce!" Rachael called out.

"Here," said Joyce, stalking out of the back of the suite. Simon noticed that she looked paler than normal, and still had her hair hanging in her face.

"What are we doing?" Simon asked.

"Got it," said Colin. "Two floors down, three rooms over. It's empty. So are the rooms on either side."

"'Three rooms over' doesn't help me," said Rachael.

"To your right, if you're facing the door."

"Okay." Rachael closed her eyes and scrunched up her lips.

"Wait," said Simon, suddenly feeling very scared, worried about what he thought was going to happen—

BOOM.

The floor shook under them. From off in the hotel, Simon could hear muffled cries.

"Mother of God, what was that?" yelled the security guard on the other side of the door. Heavy boots echoed off down the hallway.

"Let's roll," said Rachael. She opened the door, stuck her head into the hallway, looked back and forth, then motioned for everyone else to follow her.

20

YOU CAN SLEEP WHEN YOU'RE DEAD

They power walked down the hall of the hotel, brush-ing past rushing employees and guests sticking their heads out their doors. Somewhere, an alarm was whooping, and there was a faint smell of smoke in the air. Simon's mind was a smear of panic as he followed the other three. His heart pounded, his ears rang, but it was like he couldn't see, couldn't *think*, beyond getting out of there.

Rachael turned into an emergency staircase, which was cold and concrete compared to the elegant decor of the hotel around it. They pounded their way down the stairs two at a time, floor after floor, until they were almost—

"FREEZE."

Rachael stopped dead, making Simon collide into her back and Colin collide into his. A chubby hotel security guard stared daggers at them. Clutched in his outstretched hands was a large black taser.

"Okay, man, take it easy," said Rachael, holding up her palms.

"Down on the ground!" barked the officer. "NOW!"

"Colin?" asked Rachael.

"It's not online," said Colin. "Must be an old model."

"Oh, great," Rachael sighed. "Simon?"

Simon opened his mouth to respond, but couldn't say anything. He couldn't move, or think, or even use his powers. He was terrified, his heart racing and his mind reeling.

"Any day now, Simon," said Rachael.

"ON! THE! GROUND!" barked the security guard.

"Hey," said Joyce, pushing her way to the front of the crowd.

The security guard locked eyes with Joyce, and his

mouth hung open. His knees wobbled, and the taser dropped out of his hands. His eyes rolled back into his head as a dribble of drool ran down his chin—and then he collapsed in a heap.

Simon gasped. Joyce closed her eyes, took a deep breath, and said, "Come on."

Joyce headed for the stairs, with Colin and Rachael following quickly after her. Only Simon was left, staring down at the prone security guard, a feeling of sick horror rippling through his stomach.

"Simon!" called Rachael, motioning for him to follow. "Come on, we have to get out of here!"

"Is he *dead*?" asked Simon. "Rachael, did she just . . . ?"

Rachael glanced at the guard, and Simon could see she didn't care either way. She just shrugged and said, "Look, we need to leave." And then she ran, leaving Simon alone in the echoing staircase with a grown man at his feet.

Simon's breath ripped in and out of his chest as he looked at the collapsed security guard. How had this happened? He couldn't believe this. This shouldn't happen to him. He was just a kid.

No.

Rachael was right. He was more.

He closed his eyes. Took a deep breath, steadied himself. He got down on his knees and put a finger to the stubble on the man's neck.

There. A pulse.

He was still alive.

Simon reached out. Felt the man's mind, dim and lost and stuck in that horrible falling place that Joyce had pulled Simon into. He had never experienced someone like this before, when their mind wasn't present, when they had no feelings or intentions—just blankness. But he could feel the man, somewhere, mired in nothingness, fading slowly out.

Simon reached farther. Grabbed ahold of a glimmer of emotion and confusion, a flash of memories.

He wrapped his mind around it, and gently pulled upward . . .

The security guard's body jerked with a gasp. His eyes snapped open, and he stared at Simon, his body rising and falling with much-needed breaths.

"Where . . . where am I?" he mumbled.

That was all Simon needed. He took off down the stairs, out into the lobby, and through the front door.

*　　*　　*

From the street, the hotel looked like something out of the apocalypse.

A room in one corner was completely engulfed in fire, sending huge blasts of flame and thick black smoke out its shattered windows. The night sky was lit up by the gigantic, flapping blaze that billowed out of the burnt-out hole in the building. Bits of paper, glass, and charred furniture littered the streets around them. Fire engines and police cars surrounded the building, adding pulsing crimson-and-blue light to the flickering orange of the raging fire overhead. Onlookers had gathered to watch the massive blaze, staring and pointing up in the air in amazement at the sheer size of the inferno.

Simon weaved between the crowds, desperate to get away from the hotel, the fire, the look on that astonished security guard's face. He shook all over, rattled by fear. He didn't want this. He just wanted to get home, to go to bed, to wake up to his family and not worry about explosions and screams and whether or not someone lived or died—

"Simon!"

A hand landed on his shoulder. He whirled to see

Rachael standing next to him, a concerned look on her face.

"There you are," she said. "I was worried, dude. Are you okay? Man, that was a close one, right?"

Simon stared at his sister uncomprehendingly. He couldn't understand how she was this calm. And then, slowly at first but with sudden speed, he felt his teeth grind, his fists clench, and his panic turn to white-hot fury.

"You *left me there*!" he said, shoving her away.

"Okay, easy, let's not draw attention," Rachael cautioned, glancing at the onlookers nearby. "You were supposed to follow me, Simon. I didn't realize we'd lost you until I got outside."

"I had to help that security guard," he said. He heard his voice crack, and realized there were tears on his cheek, moving hot and fast. "He could've *died*, Rachael. Your friend could've killed him, for all you knew. And you just left him, and me—"

"Hey, he was going to tase me! If you'd given him a little nudge, maybe Joyce wouldn't have had to do her thing."

"Her *thing*? A *nudge*? Rachael, look at what you're doing!" Simon waved an arm out at the flaming side of the hotel and all the evacuated vacationers. "You and your friends are dangerous! How many parties is this worth?"

Rachael rolled her eyes. She turned to the burning hotel, puckered her lips, and blew like she was making a wish on a birthday cake.

The fire spewing out of the hotel vanished in an instant.

The people in the street gasped as one, and then began clapping, obviously convinced that the firefighters in the building had put out the blaze. But the stunt only made Simon feel more unsure and scared.

His sister's powers were even stronger than he'd thought. It wasn't just about starting fires, it was about *controlling* them.

Rachael turned back to Simon with a disappointed look. "How many times do I have to tell you to trust me?"

"Did you trust your creepy life-sucking friend back there when she nearly killed that guy?"

"Joyce did what she had to. It's something you're going to need to learn if you're going to roll with us. Life ain't a fairy tale, dude. Things get messy."

"Learn if—do you think I'm part of your crew

now?" Simon asked. "All I wanted to do was hang out, and you made it this, this . . . *disaster*!"

Rachael groaned and took his arm. "Look, you need to calm down. Let's just go back to the warehouse, chill out—"

"No," said Simon, shrugging her off. "No way. I'm not going anywhere with you."

"Aw, Simon, c'mon—SIMON!" Rachael called. But he was already leaving, storming away from her.

He wandered the streets of Downtown Albuquerque with no idea where he was going. He cursed himself for not bringing his phone. It was quickly becoming clear that he only knew a very small portion of the city—home, school, back—and that he had paid absolutely no attention to what bus Rachael had taken him on. He walked into a diner to ask directions, but there were TVs on every wall playing breaking news reports about the fire at the hotel, and the sight of the burning building made him turn and storm out in shame and paranoia.

In the diner parking lot, an old woman in a flannel shirt with a severe underbite offered him a ride. Simon quickly read her cloud and found no plans to kidnap him or hurt him, just pity for his current state and a painful memory of another boy, one she wished she'd stopped from leaving many years ago.

The only conversation they made on the drive was about directions—Simon guided her to his neighborhood, but not his house. As he opened the car door a few streets down from his house, the woman swatted his shoulder.

"Running away ain't never the answer, son," she said.

"Lady, you don't even know," Simon replied.

Compared with the utter chaos of downtown, his house was as dark and still as a crypt. Simon crept around back and up into his still-open bedroom window. He flopped on his bed and let out a sigh of relief.

"Hey."

Aly sat in his desk chair. She looked tired, but had a calm, understanding expression on her face.

What could he possibly say to her?

"Are you feeling better?" he asked.

"A little," she said. "I needed a moment to shut off, but I'm feeling okay. But I couldn't sleep, so I figured I'd come by, and we'd catch up."

"Oh."

"But you weren't here. So . . . where were you?"

He tried to think of a lie, but he'd never been good at lying. And with how spread thin he was after tonight, he didn't have the energy to try.

"I was with Rachael," he said.

Aly nodded slowly. "Okay. How did that go?"

He winced. "Have you checked the news lately?"

Aly shook her head. "I'm trying to stay offline for a bit. So I don't get overwhelmed. But I guess that sort of answers my question." She sighed deeply. "It's bad, isn't it?"

"It's pretty bad."

"Rachael hasn't gotten any better, has she?"

"If anything, she's worse," Simon reported. "And she's not alone."

21

NIGHTMARE LOGIC

The night went long. Simon told Aly about everything, from Lena's powers to the Franklin twins' mom to Rachael's dreams to meeting her in the warehouse and that night at the hotel. The hotel was the hardest, because he knew how disappointed Aly would be when she found out he snuck out to be with Rachael's crew. But his sister remained pretty neutral, scribbling down notes on Post-its and occasionally saying, "Then what?" or "And how did she respond?"

"Well, it definitely sounds like Rachael still needs

professional help," she said when Simon was done. "But I'm just as worried about these two others and their powers. The worst thing someone can do is tell Rachael she's right when she's in one of her moods."

"Seriously," Simon agreed. "There's something up with Joyce, too. She scares me."

"She's definitely a problem, but"—she checked her notes—"the cyberpath, Colin, is no joke, either. At any moment, he could empty Mom and Dad's bank accounts, or put us on the FBI's Most Wanted list. He could really mess up our lives."

"So why hasn't he?" asked Simon. "I mean, I'm sure Rachael could get him to. That's her superpower. Well, besides the fire thing."

"Maybe he doesn't want to," said Aly. "Maybe Rachael is right, and she and her friends are looking at a bigger picture. Maybe she's *not* coming after our family. She just wants you."

"So do I just turn her down?" he asked. "Ask her to leave town?"

Aly chewed on her lip for a moment, then shook her head. "Nah, that won't work. Rachael's never been interested in taking no for an answer. And she's come too far. She won't just go away."

"What if . . ." Simon took a deep breath. He didn't even want to say it. But every time he thought about their problem, it was one of the easier solutions. "What if I went with her? She'd leave you alone. You and Mom and Dad—"

A look of sad anger crossed Aly's face. She shook her head. "No."

"Aly, if you think about it—"

"Absolutely not," she insisted. "I am *not* losing you, too. And it's unfair to her. Rachael needs us now, too. I don't want to look for another way to run away from her. We need to be here for her. Even if that means confronting her."

"Then what's the next step?" asked Simon.

"We drop a dime," said Aly, pinching the bridge of her nose.

"We what?"

"It's an expression. We have to call the cops, Simon."

"What? No," said Simon, terror mounting in him. "Aly, I don't know if that security guard would've made it if I hadn't been there. Rachael and her friends are dangerous."

"Yeah, but that's exactly it. Rachael didn't torch

the guard immediately. That means she's not ready to just straight up kill people. From what I've seen in my research, all the buildings she's burned have been empty or evacuated. And if there are a bunch of cops, Joyce won't be able to drain them one after another. Even if she does, their cover would be blown."

As always, Aly was right. Simon considered the details, and knew that her plan actually made as much sense as anything he could imagine.

But something about it still bothered him. He couldn't say what about it worried him. But after watching Rachael snuff out a raging explosion like it was nothing, he was officially done underestimating her.

"We'll do it," he said. "But let's be careful. You never know how she might react."

"She snuck you out of here and blew up a hotel room tonight," said Aly. "Trust me, I'm very aware of what our sister's capable of."

22

WAKE-UP CALL

The way the kitchen felt now reminded Simon of his burning dream. Every second seemed to last an hour. Mom humming "Despacito" at the sink sounded tuneless and endless, trailing on in the background. His bowl of cereal sat in front of him, untouched.

He couldn't even think of eating. He felt like he was made of stone.

Any minute now, everything would change.

Finally, Aly came walking out of her room. She

seemed perfectly casual, but when she sat down, she gave Simon a quick nod. Simon inhaled sharply.

She'd put in the tip. It was done.

It was up to the cops now.

"Wait a second, young lady," said Mom, coming over to the table. "I think you might need one more day to relax. I don't want you overexerting yourself."

"I'm feeling a lot better after yesterday," Aly replied. When Mom peered suspiciously at her, she smiled back. "I'm cool, Mom. Promise."

"Well, all right," said Mom, sounding unsure. "You just take everything at a slow pace. Maybe stay offline. I worry all this social media is feeding you guys an endless stream of misery and chaos."

"I'll keep my phone in my pocket," Aly promised.

Nothing on the newswire yet, said Aly's text when Simon got to school. He checked a few local news sites, just to be sure, but didn't see anything, either.

Maybe, he dared to think, it had all gone off without a hitch. Maybe Rachael was in police custody right now, tearily calling Dad. Maybe after last night, she felt guilty or conflicted, and she just walked out of her room and surrendered herself to the cops when they raided the warehouse.

Or maybe anyone who could post anything about it is burning alive. Simon tried to banish this idea from his head. It would be okay.

He was so caught up in worrying about what would happen to his sister that he was surprised to find Lena waiting at his locker. The sight of her rattled him with guilt—he'd promised her that they'd work out a plan regarding Rachael, and instead he'd ditched Lena to cause mayhem with her.

"You never showed," Lena said softly as Simon got his books.

"I know. I'm sorry. Things escalated a little bit."

"Tell me."

"My sister came to my house last night. We went out, and . . . she blew up part of a hotel downtown."

He expected a little more amazement from Lena, but she only nodded. "I heard about that. My dad brought it up this morning."

An awful thought hit Simon. Lena's dad. The cops. "Is your dad back at work today?"

"No, he's still on leave," she said.

He heaved a sigh of relief. "Good."

"Why?"

"I can't tell you," he said. "Not yet."

Simon knew the answer wasn't enough. And from the way she glared at him, he could tell that Lena wasn't buying it.

"Let me know," she said, and darted off into the crowds.

He wandered through the day blankly, waiting for Aly's response. He stopped by the library and checked the news on the computers, but still nothing.

Maybe it would all be okay. That happened sometimes, right? If things went as bad as they often did for Simon, it would stand to reason that he was due for a stroke of good luck. Maybe this was the one time everything fell into place.

Midway through math, Nelly's "Hot in Herre" blasted from his cell phone.

"Simon, while I appreciate the music choice, ringers off in class," said their teacher, Mr. Parks.

"Sorry," said Simon, but he felt himself blanch as he reached for his phone.

That wasn't his ringtone.

Someone had changed it.

He glanced at the screen.

Video call. Unknown caller.

Might be spam.

He let it go to voicemail and put his phone on Do Not Disturb mode.

"Anyway, as I was saying," said Mr. Parks, "after isosceles triangles, you have . . . anyone? Anyone? Scalene triangles, which have—"

Simon's phone went off again.

"Really?" groaned Mr. Parks. "Simon, what'd I just say?"

Simon glanced down at his phone.

Unknown caller.

His ringer was turned back on.

He knew who it was.

"Sorry, Mr. Parks, I think it's a family emergency," grumbled Simon, hurrying out of the room. Mr. Parks cocked an eyebrow at him, but Simon couldn't be bothered to care. He stormed out into the hall and answered the call.

On his phone screen, the warehouse burned.

The entire building was engulfed, the third floor invisible for the flames that raged out of it. Firefighters stood on all sides, spraying the fire with their hoses, but it didn't seem to be making a lick of difference. Police set up wooden barricades to keep onlookers and news vans at a distance, but every so often a blast of flame would come flaring out of the warehouse and the entire crowd would shield their faces and back away, unprepared for the heat.

Simon's mouth fell open. This video had obviously been taken from a drone or a nearby rooftop, and . . .

Wait.

He peered closer at his phone.

It wasn't a video.

It was live.

The view spun, and there was Rachael glaring into the camera. She wore her cold, unfeeling expression, but Simon thought that behind it he could see a touch of hurt, a little seed of disappointment. A ways behind her, Joyce and Colin sat on a vast rooftop, looking wiped out and overheated in the sun. Wisps of smoke came off Colin, and Joyce's face was smeared with black ash.

"How many times is my family going to betray me, huh?" she asked. "How many knives am I going to have to pull out of my back?"

Simon wanted to respond, but couldn't find words.

His mouth had gone dry, and cold beads of sweat seemed to form on every part of his body at once.

"It's becoming pretty clear that I can't reinforce this bridge," she said. "And if you can't rebuild bridges, there's really only one thing to do to them."

"Rachael, listen—"

Rachael cut him off. "Be seeing you, Simon. Real soon."

She turned the phone back around to the warehouse, violently burning, the sky filled with black smoke. After a few more seconds, her call cut off, and Simon called Aly.

23

OPEN FIRE

He was sprinting for the front doors when a hand latched onto his arm. He spun, caught up in his terror, and worried that Rachael had somehow already found him.

Then he found Lena staring at him.

"I saw you running," she said. "I need to know, Simon. Now."

A million lies ran through his head at once—and none of them were as helpful as the truth. "We called the cops on Rachael, and the warehouse is burning.

She's coming for me. I have to go meet my sister and help my mom."

Lena nodded and marched past him. "I'm coming with you."

"No," said Simon, following her. "Lena, it's going to be dangerous—"

"You need all the help you can get, Simon," she said. "And she knows my face. Knows I've been in her dreams. If she gets through you, she's coming after me next. I'm in this with you."

He didn't argue. They left school and raced down the shoulder of the road on their bikes, paying no attention to the cars that sped past them. Simon couldn't be bothered to care about safety right now. All he could think about was Aly and their family.

Would the house be in flames by the time he got home? Was he already too late?

He let out a deep, relieved breath when they rounded the corner and he saw it, untouched, waiting for him down their block. They ditched their bikes in the front yard, and Simon nearly smashed his key fob trying to get inside.

Aly was already in the living room when they

arrived, talking in a calm and measured tone to Mom, who sat on the couch with a cup of coffee.

"I know I had that panic attack the other day, but that's not what this is about," Aly was saying. "Rachael is here, and she burned down a warehouse in town today. This isn't a drill."

"She's telling the truth, Mom," Simon chimed in. His mother jumped at the sight of him coming in, but seemed to read the urgency on his face as real. Lena held back, hugging herself awkwardly.

Simon went on. "She just called me. She's coming for us, and she's got some really scary people with her."

"When'd she call you?" Mom looked more frustrated than worried.

"It was just a few minutes ago." Simon checked his phone—but there was no record of the call. He looked up at Aly pleadingly. "Colin. The cyberpath. He must have manipulated it."

"*Cyberpath*," Mom sighed, shaking her head and setting down her coffee.

"This is not a joke, Mom," said Aly. "We need to call Dad, and we need to run."

"Aly, I think you're still taking this way too

personally," said Mom. "We have the police on it. They're even working with the FBI."

"Mom—"

"Do you still believe your sister can start fires with her mind?"

Aly scrunched up her face, as though she wished she'd never told her mother the truth. "Look, that doesn't matter. What matters is that we're in danger, and need to get out of here. Or at least get ready."

"If you want, I can reach out to the police and let them know you think she's behind this warehouse fire," said Mom. "But then I need you two to go back to school. You can't just leave every time you get a bad feeling about your sister."

Simon could see Aly straining to come up with something that would get across the seriousness of the situation. She bit her lip and closed her eyes, her brain racing. He hated to see her at a loss.

Simon knew a way.

He felt cold and cornered. What would Mom think? What would she say? How would she look at him afterward, knowing what he'd done, knowing what he could do?

But it might be the only way. To get her to believe, to make sure his family wouldn't burn.

Simon reached out to his mother's mind.

He expected a flood of the stone-faced frustration she was projecting . . . but what he got was worry. Heartbreak. Pain. A desperate need to hold things together, to project a sense of calm and control. Endless love for her children. Sadness at the loss of her elder daughter, and melancholy at seeing her become the villain of the family. Outright fear at how seriously her other two kids were taking this ridiculous narrative of psychic powers.

Misery. Confusion. Love in its most difficult form.

As gently as he could, Simon moved her.

Mom's hand shot out and grabbed her coffee mug off the table. She turned and whipped it at the wall on her right, where it shattered with a sharp crack and a splash of brown.

Mom and Aly stared blankly at the stain on the wall for a moment.

Now or never, thought Simon.

"I did that, Mom," he said, stepping forward. "I made you do that, with my mind. I can reach out and sense what people are thinking and feeling. And I can control certain parts of people's minds. I can make them do things—physical things. And . . . and I can hurt them if I need to."

His eyes stung, and his throat ached. But still, he forced himself to say it.

"I'm the one who put Rachael in the hospital," he said, his mouth pulling tight. Tears flew down his cheeks, but he pushed himself, hard. "She was in the school, using her powers—her *powers*, Mom, like mine, only hers are with fire. She was attacking Aly and me, and burning everything down around us. I didn't know what to do, so I . . . I pushed her. Hard. I never meant to hurt her. I don't want to hurt anyone. I just want it all to stop. And I'm sorry everything's been so crazy, and I'm sorry we couldn't tell you. But she's coming, and you need to know how real it is. How bad it is. And I'm sorry. I'm so sorry."

Before he knew it, Mom's arms were around him, and Aly's were, too, and they were all crying. He just kept saying "I'm sorry," over and over, and Mom kept shushing him as it all came rushing out.

"We're going to figure this out," Mom said. "But

it's okay. It's going to be okay. I promise. I love you so much."

"I love you, too, Mom," said Simon.

She nodded—then looked up and offered an embarrassed smile. "Oh my. Hi."

"Oh," said Simon. "Uh, Mom, this is Lena."

24

YOU MUST BE DREAMING

They sat at the kitchen table as Aly, Simon, and occasionally Lena carefully explained what had happened behind the scenes over the past year and a half. Mom listened, nodding occasionally, frowning and shaking her head here and there. Simon could see that even after his demonstration, she didn't entirely believe what she was hearing. But the way her brow furrowed occasionally let Simon know she was putting the pieces together: Aly's desk bursting into flames at their first house, the way Rachael had been able to commit so many arsons without being caught. All she was missing was one piece: that her kids weren't ordinary kids.

When they got to Dad, she refused to believe it at first.

"I've been married to your dad for seventeen years," she said. "I think I'd know if he could move things with his mind."

"Try to remember if there was a time you watched Dad open a door with his hands," said Simon. "Or closed the fridge. Or turned on the sink."

She went silent. Then she said, "Hmm."

"What?" asked Aly.

"The movie theater," said Mom. "Right before your dad proposed, we went on this date. We went to see the second *Matrix* movie. And I told my girlfriends later, that night was like a fairy tale. My drink slid into my hand, and my hoodie was zipped after I said I was cold, and our theater seats unfolded right as we walked up to them . . . it was like magic." She blushed. "I was scared to think about . . . anything like what you're saying now. So I didn't. I just told myself the universe gave me one perfect night."

"That's why he doesn't know," said Aly. "It's all small potatoes. He doesn't burn down houses or go into people's dreams or anything. He just opens the blinds and turns on the shower."

"Right." Mom's eyes snapped to Lena. "And you're serious, too. You can see what people are dreaming."

"Uh-huh," said Lena. She absently spun her thumb around the rim of her glass. She'd been silent through most of this, which Simon understood. He swore that if Lena ever revealed her powers to her parents, he'd come with her and force himself to sit awkwardly through the whole thing, for the sake of fairness.

It had gotten dark outside, with the sun leaving a shimmering orange line along the horizon. Aly got up and started turning on lights and locking doors, making the house a little less shadowy. Mom sat back, rubbed her face, and sighed.

"Okay, let's think," she said. "I'm going to keep calling your dad—I know his phone is usually off when he has a meeting, but eventually he'll pick up, and I'll tell him to come home as quickly as possible. Then we can . . . I don't know, get a hotel room or go camping or something."

As Mom got on the phone and Aly went around locking doors, Simon and Lena flopped down on the couch.

"I'm sorry about this," he said. "If you want to, you can leave. I totally understand."

She shook her head. "I'm staying. I want to do whatever I can."

Simon couldn't deny the warmth he felt at hearing her say it. "Do your parents know you're here?"

"Um . . . I think they think I'm still in school," she said. "But I'll text them once school is out and tell them I came over here. I think they're happy I have a friend."

"I know that feeling."

Mom came in then. "Okay, I reached your dad, and he says he's going to come home," she said. "For now, are you kids hungry? I can throw some of those frozen dumplings on."

Simon looked to Lena. His friend stared up at Mom, eyes wide, face blank . . . and then nodded. "Yes, please. Thank you."

Mom smiled at her, then at Simon. "Very polite, this friend of yours. You should bring her by under better—"

The lights went out around them.

"—circumstances. Oh," said Mom. She glanced around. "A blackout?"

Dread welled up in Simon. He glanced out the window across from them and saw their neighbors' house with all the lights on.

"It's not a blackout." Simon jumped to his feet. "I think it's happening. I think she's here."

"Without question," called Aly from somewhere in the house.

"You think Rachael *killed the power*?" Mom laughed. "Guys, whatever she is, Rachael's not a spy—"

"One of Rachael's friends can control any piece of machinery that's online," Simon reminded his mother. "Chances are our power is all part of a huge online network."

"Your locks, too," a voice said.

Simon froze. His skin crawled with frost.

A flame erupted in the air over the coffee table, as though an invisible ball had caught fire. In its flickering orange light, Simon saw Rachael and her friends standing at the entrance to the back hallway. And this time, Rachael's dead-eyed expression was focused right on him.

25

IF YOU DIE IN YOUR DREAM . . .

They stayed frozen. The flame continued to burn in midair, without fuel. Mom's eyes bugged out of her head at the sight. Simon didn't need to use his powers to read her mind: *So it's true after all*.

Simon started to stand, but Rachael pointed a finger and the floating flame ballooned dangerously. He sat. Lena's hand found his and clenched it.

"Cute," monotoned Rachael. "Simon, if you use your powers, I'll let Joyce take over. You want that?"

Simon dry-swallowed. "No."

"Smart kid. Mom, on the couch. Family meeting. You, too, Aly! I know you're here somewhere, trying to be clever. Out now or I torch the building and everyone in it."

As Mom sat down next to Simon and Lena, Aly came out of the kitchen with her hands up.

"There she is!" said Rachael with a big, mean smile. "Look, a traitor!"

Aly glared at Rachael with contempt. "Look, a *monster*."

"Watch your mouth, Als," snapped Rachael.

"*You* watch it, Rachael," Aly shot back. "You gonna pin this one on me, too, or is one of your new friends going to take the fall this time?"

"God, that is *so* like you," said Rachael. "Bitter little Aly, always thinks she knows best. Sit down and shut up."

"No," said Aly.

"SIT." As Rachael spoke, the ball of fire between them flared out. Simon pressed back into the couch as the heat blasted against his face and neck. "DOWN."

Aly sat, glaring at Rachael the whole time.

Rachael looked over the lineup on the couch and

huffed a breath. "Dreamgirl, go home," she said. "This is family business."

"I'm staying," said Lena.

Rachael eyed her. "Not gonna say it again, kid. You're not welcome here."

"I'm not going anywhere," Lena insisted.

"Then you're the first one to burn." Rachael raised a hand and the flame bloomed.

"Rachael, STOP." Mom leaned over, shielding Lena's body with her own. Rachael's flames sputtered and receded back to where they burned in the center of the room.

"Rach, what are you doing?" whispered Colin from behind her, eyes darting between Lena and Rachael. "You never said you were gonna—"

"Shut up, Colin," said Joyce.

"Yeah, *shut up*, Colin," spit Rachael. Her nostrils flared. "Move, Mom."

"Honey, what are you even doing here?" asked Mom, a sad look on her face. "All this, chasing us across the country, burning down these houses—*why?* What is all this for?"

"*Why?*" asked Rachael, the flame in front of her

growing. "Because you *LEFT ME THERE*! Aly and Simon left me in a hospital with *NO BRAIN*, and when I got out by myself and came home, you were just eating dinner like *NOTHING HAD HAPPENED*! And anytime I came to you, you just *LEFT*! *RAN AWAY*!"

Sweat trickled down Simon's brow. The room was hot, he now realized, hotter than Rachael's floating flame alone could've made it. Drops of condensation poured down the windows and hissed when they hit the sill. On the table, Lena's glass of water was beginning to boil.

"You scared us, Rachael," said Mom. "We didn't know you had these . . . that you could do this. We didn't know how you were feeling. And then, when you kept burning down houses, what were we *supposed* to think?"

"You were supposed to *LOVE ME*," shrieked Rachael, her voice cracking, her flame billowing.

Mom's face fell a little. "I've always loved you, honey."

Rachael's face twisted up. Her lips peeled back, revealing grinding teeth. The room got so hot, Simon thought he might pass out.

"Lies," Rachael said.

"We've never stopped loving you," continued Mom. "Not me, not your siblings, not your—"

Behind Rachael and her friends, a lock clicked, and a door opened. Rachael spun, her flame dying down to a flicker.

"Guys, I'm home!" called Dad, marching into the house. "Why's it so hot—" He froze when he saw the scene in the living room. His eyes landed on Rachael, and his face lit up with a gasp. "Rachael. Oh my God, sweetheart, you're here. We've been so worried about you."

"Sit down, Dad," snapped Rachael, pointing to his armchair.

Dad swallowed hard and said, "Rachael, I'm so happy you're home. Please, whatever this is, we can make it okay."

"I'm telling you to sit," ordered Rachael.

But Simon heard the quiver in her voice.

Dad opened his arms and stepped toward her. "I know, kiddo. I know it's been hard. Things have gotten all messed up, and you're feeling so much at once. But we can figure it out. It doesn't need to be like this." His breath hitched. "I've missed you so much. Please don't go again."

Simon watched as, for the first time that he could remember, his oldest sister turned inward.

Her shoulders hunched. Her hands clenched and unclenched. She shook her head frantically.

"No no no *no no NO*," she wailed. "You'll leave me, and I'll be here again, and there'll be nothing else left, *nothing else*—"

"Please, kiddo," said Dad. "I'm sorry I wasn't there for you."

The corners of Rachael's mouth turned down at the edges.

"Oh, Daddy," she sobbed.

Dad took another step forward, a smile crossing his face.

Joyce stepped into his arms.

"Excuse me, who're—" Dad froze midsentence. He took a deep, shaking breath . . . and then his eyes rolled back, his mouth fell open, and he collapsed into a heap.

"Dad!" screamed Simon.

"Wait, stop!" cried Rachael. "Joyce, what are you—"

Joyce spun on Rachael and glared at her. Rachael blinked, and screamed. For a brief moment, she seemed to know what was happening, and fire exploded around the two of them in a roar—but then it died, and Rachael fell to the floor, white-eyed and limp.

"Rachael!" Mom started forward—but Joyce flung out a hand, and Mom flew back against the couch. She threw out another, and the flame over the coffee table burst back to life with furious power.

"Don't worry," said Joyce, her eyes glowing with flickering firelight. "You'll see her again soon."

26

WAKE UP DEAD

"You . . . you killed her!" cried Simon, looking at his sister's limp form on the ground.

"Not yet," Joyce replied, "but I'm getting there." Her body heaved deep breaths. Simon could see that something had changed in her. She no longer looked sickly and weak; instead, her muscles looked strong and tight, her hair healthy and flowing, her expression full of confidence and power. Something about sapping Dad and Rachael had made her stronger.

"What'd you do to them?" shouted Mom.

"I took them." Joyce flicked a hand, and the coffee table flew across the room and crashed into the wall. She flicked the other, and the floating flame grew and swirled with beautiful spirals of fire. "And they gave me a little something in return. For now, anyway. It'll wear off. It always does."

"Joyce, don't do this," whispered Colin, who stood shivering with his back against one wall. "Please, we don't need to—"

"Do you want me to leave, Colin?" snapped Joyce without looking at him. "Do you want to be all alone out there again? With no one? *Nothing?*" Colin hid his face in his hands. "That's right. Now hush."

"And I thought Rachael was bad," mumbled Aly.

"What are you?" asked Simon, realizing what Joyce had done. "An energy parasite? Some kind of vampire?"

Joyce coughed a laugh without smiling. "*Vampire.* So stupid. You still don't get it, Simon. I'm just a kid like you, or your sister, or your dad. Nature gave me an ability no one else has." A dark cloud seemed to pass over her expression. "But it's also killing me. If I stop using my powers . . . well, you saw in the bathroom."

"I'm sorry," said Lena.

Joyce shrugged. "We do what we have to. But normal people, they're not enough. People like you, like *us* . . . when I take them, it helps. I get better, *really* better. It just never lasts. So when I met Rachael, and heard about this whole family of people like me, I thought maybe this would be it. Maybe with enough power, I could make it stop. I could close the hole." She glanced at Lena. "I didn't even know about you, Lena. Maybe, if this works, you can come with me and Colin on the road. First, though, I need your friend. And his sisters."

"You leave my kids alone," snapped Mom, furious tears coursing down her cheeks. "If you want them, you'll have to go through me."

"Fine," said Joyce. "That'll be quick."

"Wait!"

Aly leapt to her feet.

"I want to go first," she said.

"Fine," said Joyce. "Doesn't matter. You'll all come with me eventually."

Aly ran in front of Joyce and threw her arms wide. "I'm ready. Let's go."

Joyce stepped forward, grabbed Aly's shoulders, and stared deep into her eyes.

And stared. . . . and stared.

"You done?" asked Aly.

"What . . . what is this," whispered Joyce. She let go of Aly and took a step back.

"Oh, did Rachael not tell you about *my* power?" asked Aly. "See, my mind's a steel box. No one can get inside it. Or take anything from it."

She took a step toward Joyce. The blond girl backed up, suddenly unsure. She flung out her hand, and Aly seemed to be blown back a little . . . but still took another step. The floating flame blazed, blackening the ceiling, but Aly didn't seem to notice.

"Aw, is my dad's power already wearing off?" Aly went on. "That's the thing about my power—it's not flashy, like Rachael's or my dad's. Honestly, it's kind of a bummer as a psychic ability, right? Except this way, when everyone's reading minds and going into dreams, they can't get to me. But I can get to *them*. Like *THIS*."

Aly swung her right fist up into Joyce's jaw.

Joyce whirled, staggered, and hit the floor.

The lights came on. The floating flame died, but the ceiling was burning. Simon ran into the kitchen and grabbed their fire extinguisher—one of the family's six around the house, after the year they'd had—out from under the sink. When he came back into the room, Colin yanked it out of his hands.

"Help your family," he said, and immediately began spraying the ceiling.

Mom was at Rachael's side, shaking her and desperately saying her name over and over. Simon ran to Dad, reached out with his powers . . . and found him, falling endlessly, flailing in the void.

Simon raised him. The moment Dad woke with a gasp, Simon moved over to Rachael.

His mind reached deep into her mind, and found her just the same, plummeting and lost. But when he tried to take hold of her, a searing sensation stabbed at his skull and the back of his throat. As though his brain were being singed.

The fire. Rachael's power. It was fighting back, defending her and itself against intruders.

No. He wouldn't let go. Not again.

Simon grabbed ahold of Rachael and felt the inside of his brain burn. He pulled, hard. Without meaning to, he screamed.

Rachael shot up, coughing out a cloud of smoke. Mom gasped, and clutched her tighter. Dad crawled over to her and held on to one of her hands. Rachael's eyes scanned the room, and she groaned.

"Aw, my huge supervillain moment got totally messed up," she said. "*Now* what am I going to do?"

"PBFFFT."

They all looked at Lena. She had a hand over her mouth, and was shaking her head as though to say, *Sorry, never mind, that was inappropriate*, but then another laugh erupted from between her lips, and soon her whole body was shaking with laughter. And as the wail of sirens and the shouting of police swelled in the background, Simon found himself joining in, relieved beyond measure, laughing along with her.

27

SLEEP WITH ONE EYE OPEN

The room felt like a doctor's office. Everything was painted a harmless blue, and there was padding over any surface against which one could bump or bash their head. Simon sat on one side of a big linoleum desk with a lamp. On the far wall was a poster of a purple *Triceratops* riding a hoverboard in space, emblazoned with the words *Reading Is Far-Out*.

Still creepy, though. Simon could feel how sterile and inhuman the place was, a room meant for business of a sensitive nature. He'd known a room like this was in his future as soon as his family had been transferred from the cops to the officials in suits with the armed black ops–looking bodyguards.

It was only a matter of time before someone found them.

There was one of the security officers outside his room now, he knew. He could feel that the guy was there, could sense his presence, but couldn't read what was going on inside his brain. The fact that whoever was standing out there had something similar to Aly's power made him especially worried. They were officially in over their heads.

The door finally opened, and a woman in a business skirt and blouse stepped inside. She had a huge file cradled under her arm with what looked like a big medieval *M* on it.

"With oat milk, please," she called out the door. "Sorry, did you hear me? Well, then, what'd I ask for? Oat milk. Thank you." She closed the door and sat down across from Simon, all smiles. "I'm sorry you had to wait. These things always take forever."

Simon didn't respond. He'd decided that he'd tell these goons as little as he possibly could.

"Simon, right?" she asked.

"I'm sure it's all in your file," Simon replied.

"It is!" she chirped, and flipped open the file. "Look at that. Simon Theland, age eleven, born in Philadelphia, Pennsylvania, last known residence Albuquerque, New Mexico. Wow, you're big for eleven! Eleven-year-olds must come bigger these days." She flipped the page. "And it says here you've got extraordinary telepathic abilities, which have earned you a . . . C-5 rating. Which isn't *THAT* bad, but obviously has everyone at our organization very interested."

"And who is your organization?" he asked.

"Well, I'm with Virgo, who'll be handling your case file," said the woman. "I'm Joanna, by the way, and I'll be your direct contact. I'm who you call if you, I don't know, accidentally destroy your house with your powers. We'll open up a claim."

"And then what? Dissect our brains? Train us to fight wars for you?"

"What am I, made of money?" Joanna laughed. "Kiddo, surgery and military training are very expensive, and this is a government organization. We're painfully underfunded. And from what I'm seeing, you're . . ." She consulted her file. "A pretty good kid, right? You've had one or two recent outbursts. This thing at the street fair is pretty ugly. But you're not planning any terrorist activity, right?" She peered at the paper and smiled. "And look at you, saving this hotel security guard. Well done, Simon."

Simon's cheeks heated up. He told himself it was the weirdness of being watched by some shady government organization and not feeling pride over doing what anyone in his shoes would've done.

"Point is, we have no reason to detain you," she said, closing the file. "We're definitely gonna put a chip in your hand, though, and if you have other outbursts, we have to check in with you about them, and you might have to talk to a shrink from Gemini. But right now, we've got bigger fish to fry. Like your sister."

"If you think Rachael's going to cooperate with you, you're dreaming," said Simon.

"Rachael?" Joanna peeked in the file. "Look at that, you have *two* sisters! And Rachael is a . . . oh, pyrokinetic. She's a C-4, not much more worrisome than you. Ha! C-4!" She grinned at him, and waited. "C-4? Explosives? Pyro? No? Nothing? You'll get it later. Right before you fall asleep. Anyway, nasty outburst record, but we were all fifteen once. No, I'm talking about Alysson here. She's a B-3."

"Aly? Aly's harmless. Her mind's just a wall."

"Aly's a ticked-off middle child with a very useful ability. A lot of bad people are interested in a unique person like that. We need to keep a close eye on her."

"Like your security guard out there?"

Joanna grinned. "That's actually a helmet they wear, but the guys in Aries will be really excited that you think it feels like the real thing."

"What about Lena?" he asked. "And Rachael's friends?"

"Lena is the . . . somnipath? Dream infiltration?" Joanna flipped through the file. "Yeah, says here she's free to go. The other kids . . . Colin Molina, held for questioning, and Joyce Pilkers, held for questioning. That's all I know, but that makes sense. Looks like Colin is a pretty powerful cyberpath."

"And Joyce?" Simon asked.

Joanna looked at him for a moment, and sighed. "Real talk, kid? We don't have a name for her yet. But whatever her power is doing to her body is really nasty, and her family situation is not good. So we're gonna try to help her with those before anything else."

Simon sighed. He was terrified of Joyce, after what he'd seen. She'd dismantled both Dad and Rachael in a matter of seconds, and then used their powers like she'd had them her entire life. But what was even scarier was that he couldn't even really blame her.

Just a kid like you. That's what she'd told him.

What if his powers had started eating him alive? What would he have done?

"Anything else?" Joanna asked. "Any other questions?"

Simon thought for a moment. "How many of us?"

"In the world?" asked Joanna. "I think about seventeen million?"

"Whoa."

"Yeah, most are like your dad, and don't know it," she said with a shrug.

He thought some more. "C-5?"

"Right, so you're pretty solidly in the middle," she said. "It's the A's you really have to watch out for."

"Is there an Area 51?" he asked.

"No," said Joanna.

"What about Bigfoot? And Dracula. Is Dracula real?"

"You know your family is out there, right?" Joanna non-answered with a smile. "They might want to see you."

28

DREAM COME TRUE

It's all here at once.

The scene is the same, but every step, every second, brings in parts of the past few weeks. Their old oven sits next to their New Mexico fridge. Aly's running at his side, and then it's Colin crying, and then it's a police officer yelling at them to get in the van. Behind him looms Rachael, only now her flaming gorgon's face is crying tears of lava, and Dad's hugging her, and there's a dark shape in the distance, pitch-black, with fluttering hair and huge, glowing eyes . . .

The fridge flies open. A blinding flash of light. Simon covers his eyes.

When he puts his hands down, he's in the desert, dusty and endless.

In front of him sits an old theater, vine wrapped and abandoned, its tall black windows empty and haunting. Simon looks in all directions, and sees the mountains in the distance, but no other trace of life. It's just the desert, the theater, and him.

Simon walks up the creaking stairs, past the box office with its scattered tickets, and into the darkened front hallway. The walls on either side of him are lined with classic posters, only Lena has taken center stage on all of them. There's Lena in a cocktail dress and wide-brimmed hat, stealing a diamond. There's Lena in a suit of armor, eyes turned up to God as she leads French Crusaders into battle.

There's Lena leaving a mausoleum, arms extended, surrounded by rotting corpses rising from their graves. Beneath her is a title in dripping letters: THE ZOMBIE.

The theater is vast and empty; a large crack in its high ceiling lets in a blade of gray daylight. The walls are decorated with blurred, warped scenes, like a classical painting rendered with an AI program. Angels look down with smeared faces and chariots with blurred wheels ride around coliseums full of expressionless stand-ins. The stage itself is a dingy open mouth, its lip coated in dust and its curtains rotting in huge, dangling sections.

From past the stage, he hears a door open.

He goes backstage and up a creaky spiral staircase. He passes a floor that's entirely taken up by racks of costumes, overflowing with feather boas and hoop skirts and robes and trousers. He recognizes the spiked leather jacket, the flowing white skirt, the vest.

The staircase ends in a door reading PRIVATE.

Simon knocks.

"Come in."

The top floor of the theater is empty except for a big fluffy couch, a standing lamp, a vanity with a mirror, and a small shelf full of books. Across from him, at one of the tall, glassless windows spilling light into the space, sits Lena. He goes over to her and sits down next to her; even though he knows this is just a dream, he feels a twinge of dangerous glee as he lets his sneakers dangle out into the air next to her cowboy boots.

More than anything, though, he is overjoyed to

see her. To know that she's okay, and that he can still find her here.

The empty desert and the brown sandy mountains yawn at them.

"Welcome," says Lena.

"Thanks for having me," says Simon. "How are you?"

"I'm okay. They basically asked me a lot of questions about you guys, and how I've used my powers in the past, and whether or not I've ever used them on, like, a president or something like that. Then they did an MRI on me and sent me home. The most painful part was getting the chip."

"Yo, for real." Simon remembers the shooting pain as they pressed the tiny metal square under the skin of his hand. He reaches down, but all he feels is the web between his thumb and pointer. "Huh, I don't have the chip in my dream."

"Really? I have mine." Lena raises her hand and shows off the dark square in her skin.

"Weird," says Simon.

"Super weird," says Lena.

"Did you get in any trouble with your folks?"

"Yeah, but they were more scared than angry. My dad apparently drove around looking for me."

"I'm sorry," says Simon. "I'm sorry for everything, Lena. I didn't know it would go down like that."

She shrugs and smiles. Flicks her fingers and then she's holding a Coke. She takes a sip and hands it to Simon.

"You know, I'm actually okay with it," she tells him. "Or no, not okay with it. I'm pretty freaked out by it. But I don't have a lot of experiences like this, out here, and this . . . this was important. Being your friend has taught me a lot, Simon. So thank you."

"So we're still friends," he says with a heave of relief. He sips the Coke, which tastes like every Coke he's ever had rolled into one.

"Well . . . I don't know." She squints at the mountains. Flicks her fingers, and they have snow on them. Then she turns to him with a sad sigh.

"My brother came up with the 'Lena the Zombie' name at a sleepover with his friends," she says. "Because they caught me staring off into space, like I do. And then, somehow, through someone's brother, it crept into our school, and one day people there started calling me that. And that night, when I came here, that poster downstairs was up. I didn't do that consciously, it just showed up. So that night, I went into my brother's dreams, and I rose from the dead with a bunch of other zombies. And we ripped him to pieces."

Simon feels a crush of nausea. "Whoa."

She nods. "Then I woke up, because he was crying so loudly in the next room. The next day, he wouldn't speak to anyone. I've never felt so bad in my life. So while I like being your friend, I think I have miles to go before I sleep. I may have to take things one day at a time."

"Fair enough," says Simon.

They watch the horizon for a bit longer, and then Lena stands and dusts off her butt.

"Not to invite you over and then kick you out, but I've got some thinking to do," she says.

"All good." Simon stands. "So . . . see you at school?"

"Guess so," she says.

Simon stares at her a bit, and she stares back. He doesn't want to leave. He wishes there was something else he could say.

"Tell you what," he ventures. "If you want to hang out, or if you want me to come over and talk to you, or whatever, just give me a sign, okay? Something that lets me know."

Lena smiles. "That's fun. Okay, deal. And same."

"Cool." Simon stands there a moment longer and then realizes: "I don't know how to wake up. I've never done it myself before."

"Here, let me help," says Lena.

She grabs the front of Simon's shirt and throws him out the window.

"Oh, thanks a lot!" he calls as he plummets toward the dirt.

On the day they returned to school, Aly got up early and ate with him. They didn't talk much, but having her there felt good, and he could tell that she felt the same way. It reminded him of the days when he couldn't get out of bed or get dressed on his own, and she'd brought him breakfast and talked him through it.

What a memory. That all felt like a million years ago.

Mom and Dad came out looking professional and buttoned down, and said they were off to their first therapy session with Rachael at the holding facility.

"Eventually, they're going to want you guys to

come with," said Dad. "No pressure, but I think it's a good idea."

"I'll think about it," said Aly.

Rolling up to school after the past four days was like returning to Earth after visiting space. Simon felt like he could smell every pencil eraser and hear every skidding sneaker at once when he walked into the halls. He got one or two side-eyes from people who still knew him as the weird kid, and who'd maybe heard about the fire at his house. But otherwise no one cared. He locked eyes with Ariana Franklin as he passed her, and she gave him a silent but hard nod.

Lena was in history class when he got there. When she saw him, she turned in her seat.

Crossed her cowboy boots in front of her.

Simon couldn't have stopped himself from smiling if he'd tried. He took the desk next to hers without a word.

"They're even cooler in real life," he said.

"They're giving me terrible blisters," she said. She looked into Simon's eyes and smiled back at him. "Hey, friend."

"Hey," he said, heart bursting, mind racing.

* * *

"Wake up, Joyce."

Joyce's eyes open. She doesn't know where she is. The light overhead is red.

As she sits up on the white bench, Joyce notices the change in her body immediately. She is strong. No, not strong—just not weak. There is no tension pulling at her core, no softness in her joints and head, no feeling of a phantom creature inside of her taking its cut of her energy.

She feels fine. Healthy, even.

Which means something is very wrong.

On the other side of the room sits a woman in a black dress with her hands linked over her stomach. Behind her stands a fat older man in a brown suit, whose thick glasses make his eyes look huge. The woman shows no fear, but he is terrified.

"Where am I?" Joyce asks through a sore, dry throat.

"You're in a questioning facility, Joyce," says the woman. "My name is Dr. Kerrier, and I work with the Aquarius division. Behind me is my colleague, Mr. Manitoba, from Taurus."

Joyce feels sluggish, but not in a bad way. Her body is fluid and graceful. Her movements seem to . . . *flow*.

"Is this a dream?" she asks, staring at her own hand, testing this sensation.

"No," says Dr. Kerrier. "This is real, Joyce."

"Then what's happening to me?" asks Joyce.

"The light overhead is special," says Dr. Kerrier. "It's feeding the energy well inside of you at a steady rate. This should combat the weakness you normally feel due to your powers."

Joyce shudders.

A well.

Daddy had called her that. In the hospital parking lot, after the doctors couldn't find anything wrong with her for the third straight visit. She'd been walking up ahead, him and Mama behind, "whispering" so loud the whole neighborhood could hear them.

It's like throwing money down a well. And she ain't never gonna get any better. Why are we even doing this?

"Joyce, as I'm sure you know, you are a young woman of exceptional talents," contines Dr. Kerrier. "Our parent organization is interested in exploring them. However, thus far, your own powers have come with a downside. If you don't feed them, they feed on you."

"Thus far?" asks Joyce.

Dr. Kerrier smiles. "We'd like to fix your condition, Joyce. To stop your powers from attacking your body. Then we'd like to hear everything you learned about the Theland children while living with your friend Rachael. And after that, we would like to have you run some exercises to determine what you're capable of when your body is not being drained from the inside out."

Joyce breathes, long and slow. Two years on the road. Eating scraps from the trash, until she met Colin. Keeping him tethered and sad, scared that she'd leave him. Then Rachael, then this whole mission to find Rachael's family and drink them all down at once . . . all so she can get better.

And here it is, all out in front of her. A solution. A future.

All she has to do is walk away from her life.

Finally.

"Will I ever see my family again?" asks Joyce.

Dr. Kerrier frowns. "I'm afraid not, Joyce."

"Good," says Joyce. "Then I'm in. What do you want to know about Rachael?"

ACKNOWLEDGMENTS

Thanks as always to my editor, David; my agent, John; my mom, Anna; my brother, Quin; and my sister, Maria.

Thanks to my aunt Theresa, for always pushing me to be a weirdo, and my uncle Dan, for all the comics.

Thank you, Azara, for every day. Thank you, Jacob, for everything.

It would be silly to write a book about dreams and not mention Neil Gaiman. The stories in the *Sandman* graphic novels shaped and throttled me as a young reader; without them, I would not be here, writing this. The universal absurdity of dreaming is something Gaiman showed me in vivid detail, and there's a lot of that in this book. Here's a glass to him, at some old tavern with a centaur, because c'mon, there's always some centaur bartender in a Neil Gaiman story.

ABOUT THE AUTHOR

Christopher Krovatin is an author and journalist whose YA and middle-grade novels include *Ablaze, Awake, Darkness, Red Rover, Heavy Metal & You, Venemous, Frequency*, and the Gravediggers trilogy. His work for publications including MetalSucks, *Kerrang!*, *Revolver*, The Pit, and Invisible Oranges has made him an expert on art that would make anyone feel like they could start a fire with their mind.

Chris currently lives in Bethlehem, Pennsylvania, with his wife, Azara, and their son, Jacob. He would love to know what you're going to be for Halloween.